CRIMINAL CONVERSATION

NICOLAS FREELING

CRIMINAL CONVERSATION

VINTAGE BOOKS
A Division of Random House
New York

First Vintage Books Edition, March 1981
Copyright © 1966 by Nicolas Freeling
All rights reserved under International and Pan-
American Copyright Conventions. Published in
the United States by Random House, Inc., New
York. Originally published by Harper & Row,
Publishers, New York, in 1966.

Library of Congress Cataloging in Publication Data
Freeling, Nicolas.
Criminal conversation.
Reprint of the ed. published by Harper & Row,
New York.
I. Title.
[PR6056.R4C7 1981] 823'.914 80-6127
ISBN 0-394-74692-9

Manufactured in the United States of America

CRIMINAL CONVERSATION

PART ONE

1

VAN DER VALK WAS TIRED and a little irritable. Lately there seemed to have been happening at Central Recherche—the criminal investigations department in the city of Amsterdam—an unusual number of silly things. Time-wasting, fruitless, inconsequential. He could at least congratulate himself that the department did not have to deal with fiscal frauds, which were sent to a small special squad headed by a chief inspector with an economics degree. "The economical gentlemen," Commissaris Samson, the departmental chief, called them; he didn't like them either. Technically, Chief Inspector Kan and Inspector Scholten were both senior to Van der Valk, but secretly Mr. Samson got on better with Van der Valk because, like him, he wasn't a gentleman either.

They had all been pestered by an upheaval in what

3

the papers persisted in calling the underworld. The public adores reading about the underworld, which is so colorful, especially when the reporters put in the colorful nicknames, and if there aren't any, they make some up. The police prefer things to be less colorful.

Rita the Eyebrows, so called because she shaved hers off, had come in and denounced, for reasons of her own, a well-known "figure of the underworld" as the man who had assaulted the Greek. It was all the Greek's fault, really; why had the fellow been tedious enough to die of his injuries? Now, with an absolutely cut-and-dried formal accusation, they had to arrest Cross-Eyed Janus. They confronted him with Rita, who promptly retracted everything. She explained that Kurt the Mouse, Janus's great pal, would do her in if it was known that she had ratted on a comrade. She was told in return (a) that the lawyers disliked anonymous denunciations, and (b) that Kurt was serving a two-year stretch for armed assault resulting in grave bodily harm, plus possession of illegally acquired firearms.

After much tactful reasoning, Rita had been encouraged to build up her case again. Contrary to the sentimental imaginings of the public, prostitutes are not desperately unhappy, nor do they in the least grudge giving eighty percent of their earnings to a protector. Rita had simply not forgiven Janus for telling everybody that it wasn't only her eyebrows that were shaved.

She'd repeated her story in front of the judge of instruction. Papers had gone to the prosecutor, a case had been prepared, Janus—grinning in his inimitable cross-eyed way—had been produced. And the bitch had

4

gone right back on everything in court, and Janus had had to be freed, for lack of full and convincing establishment of the painstakingly prepared indictment.

"And the next person who comes in here with a denunciation of anybody," shouted Van der Valk, greatly annoyed, "I'll have arrested for indecent exposure!" He was not pleased when in the next morning's mail a letter was found accusing Dr. Hubert van der Post of doing away with a certain Cabestan, an elderly alcoholic painter who had recently been found dead in his flat; the cause of death, admittedly, seemed a bit vague.

And Chief Inspector Kan was on leave again—sick leave, too. With piles, adding insult to injury. Van der Valk put up with Kan well enough, for he was a dry stick and a conscientious, loyal person, but Van der Valk suspected him of making altogether too good a thing out of this. He read the letter twice and dragged unwillingly in to Mr. Samson.

Mr. Samson was working, which was something of a rarity. He had sworn to get Cross-Eyed Janus even if it gave him piles, too. For in the last two years the only thing they had ever really been able to pin on the horrible fellow was three months, for altering an automobile license with intent to defraud. The heat got so insistent that a lucrative business as importer of unroadworthy German motorcars (religiously paying excise duties on scrap metal) had dried up. Mr. Samson was searching for singeing five-year indictments in his lawbook; Van der Valk put the letter on the desk without comment. The Commissaris came swimming up from his vengeful train of thought, pushed his glasses back on his nose, and moved his eyes enough to reach the corner of the desk. He didn't react as Van der Valk had hoped he would, with the stubby finger pointing at the wastepaper basket.

"What you doing right now?" Samson asked.

"I'm very very busy," said Van der Valk.

"What with?"

"A fellow let his auto fall in the canal. When the fire crane got it out, they found six thousand pornographic magazines in the luggage compartment."

"You don't call that being busy?"

"You mean take this fellow up on his suggestion? You mean it?" Van der Valk asked.

"Why not?"

"We'll only look foolish."

"We do anyway," said Mr. Samson disagreeably.

There just wasn't anything Van der Valk could do to get out of it. It was Kan's work, really. Damn Kan.

Back in his office, he read the letter again. It was a decidedly queer letter.

DEAR SIR,

I have no doubt that you attach little weight to anonymous denunciations. I would be ready to abandon anonymity if I can receive certain assurances. I will make these known, together with the conclusions I have reached regarding the death of a certain Cabestan, to a responsible police officer. If the department has no interest, I will trouble it no further. If on the other hand the police is interested to hear that the author of this death is certainly Dr. Hubert van der Post, a responsible officer can meet me on the steps of the Amstel Hotel at ten-fifteen in the morning precisely on the day this letter is received.

He can identify himself by dropping a copy of the Frankfurter *Allgemeine Zeitung*.

Van der Valk looked at his watch. It was nine-fifteen. He toyed with the idea of having this ingenious gentleman picked up and shadowed to his home or place of business, so that his identity could be studied at leisure. Then he grinned. Talking about "the department" in that toffee-nosed way . . . an anonymous letter in a discursive, elaborate, self-important style that was rare. Faintly interested, Van der Valk decided to do the job himself. The pornographic magazines were not all that amusing.

He had ten minutes to wait, which he spent reading the Frankfurter *Allgemeine Zeitung,* his interest growing fainter. But at ten-fifteen exactly an elderly thin man of distinguished appearance left the hotel abruptly, paused on the step, and looked sharply about. Van der Valk dropped his newspaper on the step obediently. The man walked straight up to him and said, "I have a taxi waiting," in a frosty patrician voice.

Van der Valk picked up his newspaper, trotted along, and got in meekly.

"Javakade." A decided tone; the taxi got into gear in an unhurried way. The man did not speak; he spent his time looking out of the rear window. Van der Valk looked at him. Long bony face, grayish-colored. Expensive gray suit. Correct flat silver hair. Eyes, nose, and mouth accustomed to oversee, preside over, and, if need be, dominate the Annual General Meeting. A narrow man perhaps, obstinate, opinionated, but with decision and intelligence.

He had been wondering what on earth was to be

found at the Javakade, a long, deserted-looking wharf in the docks where the East Indian trade had flourished in the days of Holland's empire. Suddenly he tumbled to it; not bad. To reach the docks, an auto traveling from central Amsterdam has to cross a whole puzzle of waterways and inlets, over swing or bascule bridges, where traffic is slow and reduced to a single-line trickle. It is a simple matter to see whether any other auto on the road has business on the Javakade, where the dock forms a dead end.

"That'll do here, driver. Wait for me five minutes." They got out, walked around a corner, and stood on the wharf.

"Who are you?" asked the patrician voice.

"My name is Van der Valk. It so happened that I opened the mail this morning. This card identifies me." A sharp look.

"I suppose I can at least be grateful that you haven't tried to have me followed. Are you ready to listen to me? To treat what I have to say in confidence at least until I have made myself clear? Very well. If you agree, we will go back into the town."

The taxi started again abruptly; if the driver was curious, he wasn't trying hard. They drove back as far as the station, where the gray man got out, paid the taxi, and, without looking at Van der Valk, walked calmly, neither slow nor fast, over the bridge, where a row of autos stood parked along the water. He unlocked a prudish black Rover and motioned the policeman in. There was a good smell of blond leather. The sun slid out from behind a cloud, looked at Amsterdam without any great enthusiasm, and slid back in again.

8

"That all seemed rather childish to me," said Van der Valk indifferently. "Waste of a good taxi, I call it. The driver would recognize you, if called upon."

"That does not interest me," levelly. "I wished to see whether you would have me followed, which would have shown a police mentality, and that I would have found a kind of bad faith. If you had wished, without listening to me, to know who I was and all about me, I should have refused to speak to you. Sharing my taxi has no legal meaning whatever."

"These legal tricks bore me. You ask me to keep an appointment; I keep it. Of course I want to know who you are and why you write me a peculiar letter; otherwise I would not be here. It would have been quite normal if I had detailed a man to follow you. Since you ask for my interest, why be surprised at my taking an interest? Why pretend that you didn't write the letter? If you won't go further with the accusations you hint at being able to support, why write it at all? Why waste my time and yours?"

The gray man gave a very thin smile indeed. "I am a businessman, Mr. van der Valk. I am proud of the fact that in all my career I have never done anything unethical, or even questionable. It has, however, frequently been my experience to meet unethical persons, even to do business with them. I am a cautious person; perhaps that is why I am successful. Both the letter and the taxi were a kind of test. I was prepared at any time to break off my overtures. I still am."

"I will listen to what you say. I will receive it in confidence until I know exactly what is being asked of me. I will then give you an honest opinion. Is that what you want?"

"Yes, Mr. Van der Valk. I do not impute a lack of ethics to you, but this is, if I may call it so, a case of conscience. What do you do when you know that a person is a criminal, when you even have absolute certainty, but when you lack effective proof?"

Sadly, Van der Valk thought about Cross-Eyed Janus. This was what you might call a slightly different milieu, but the results seemed to be the same.

"We use patience. Proof is a thing that may be furnished in unlikely ways."

"Just so. I have no proof of whatever I can allege."

"But you have certainty, if I have understood you?"

"You may judge of that. I will not lay myself open to any charge of malicious falsehood. My word has never been questioned; it is not going to be now. You may act or not, as you think fit, on what I have to say, but I will make no formal accusation. I will not have my name brought forward. If proof is supplied, it is for you to supply it. Are you so surprised that I should have scruples, that I should hesitate to give my name before being satisfied that a man of responsibility and intelligence was prepared to respect my words? Do you think that a man like me is going to walk up the steps of a police bureau, give his card to the first man he sees in a uniform, and blurt out a damaging tale that carries weight simply because it comes from a man accustomed to weigh his words to the first nonentity with sufficient years of service to give him a seat behind a desk? I wrote my anonymous letter deliberately, doubtful whether you would react at all. Since you have, it encourages me to believe I may be able to go a step further, but it is not too late, Mr. van der Valk, to remain strangers to one another."

10

Van der Valk, impassive during all this, took out a cigarette, lit it, turned a little toward the man next to him, and leaned his elbow on the leather back rest.

"You are a tortuous person," he said. "You wish to make an accusation but wish not to be responsible for making it. So you think up all this, wishing and hoping, I have no doubt, to excite my curiosity and thereby secure my interest. That was, I think, the real purpose of this taxi game. Very well, I can understand all this. You are not happy because you think your accusation may have no value, even that I might think you are activated by malice. Let's cut all this out. If *I* think there is nothing in what you may think or know, I will forget this conversation. I will not even try to pierce your identity. If I think action is needed, I will take the responsibility of acting, and your name will not be disclosed till proof is found—if it is found. Will that satisfy you of my good faith?"

"Yes. You are obviously an intelligent person."

"If you had chosen, you could have told me all that you knew in a letter, and still remained anonymous. Leaving me the decision whether to act or not."

"The tale involves members of my family. But aside from that incidental fact, this is a grave allegation. If I make it, I make it in person. I am not a street-corner informer." Where, wondered Van der Valk, does pomposity become dignity?

"You know," Van der Valk said heavily, "you are asking a great deal of me."

"That is true. You will also see that I am asking a lot of myself. It would have been a great deal more in my interest to have kept silent. That silence would, however, have been guilty. I would have become a conniver."

"I think the time has come when I should know your name," Van der Valk said. Curious, he was thinking—even comic. A bond exists between this very stiff, very rich, very careful character and Shaved Rita.

"My name is Carl Merckel. I am a merchant banker. I am the managing director of the firm of Lutz Brothers."

These short sentences irritated Van der Valk very much. He realized instantly that he was on treacherous ground. This man was one of the half-dozen most important men in Holland. Fingers in all the important affairs, financing numerous state projects, with a whole portfolio of Ministers and state secretaries in his left trouser pocket. He could, if he had wished, put the whole police apparatus in motion without his name ever appearing at all. He had not done so. Van der Valk respected this man, but that did not check his irritation. A man who, last night at the Amstel Hotel, had sat at table at a formal dinner with the Minister of Justice, a Royal Highness, two directors of the Netherlands Trading Company, and the burgomaster of Amsterdam.

"I know your name, of course," Van der Valk said. "I know your friends. Why did you not go to them with your story?"

Mr. Merckel disregarded this without moving his face. Cold eyes bored into the highly polished wood that paneled his dashboard.

"I am talking to you in a parked auto," he said curtly. "I have not asked you to come to my house or

12

to my office, and I should be grateful if you will not at any time come to see me at either. I will give you a telephone number. Now, to the point."

Van der Valk lit another cigarette and leaned back. Inside the range of his eye and ear streetcars clanked and autos tooted, bicycles clattered and people chattered—the New Side Voorburgwal, one of Amsterdam's dreariest, dustiest streets. It was devoted to newspaper offices and advertising agencies, secondhand bookshops that look seedy and cafés that seem always to be empty. The doors were covered with dust and peeling paint; the pavement was littered with garbage cans that still had not been taken in, and the access to the public lavatory was completely blocked by bicycles in varying stages of decay. Locked in a smell of expensive leather and fine machinery, he felt a strong sense of unreality.

"A man came to see me, not long ago, whom I once knew slightly, because many years ago, at a time when he was a fashionable painter, I had commissioned him to do a portrait of my first wife. This man was called or called himself Casimir Cabestan. He wished, he said, to paint my second wife, who is a very good-looking woman. I refused. He then came out with a most confused tale, full of vague hints and veiled threats, which I judged to be an effort at blackmail. I spoke to him sharply."

Ah, thought Van der Valk, I think you well capable of that.

"He claimed that my wife was conducting an affair with a doctor she has consulted, that he had found this out—how he did not say—and that he deserved, he seemed to think, a reward for telling me. I told him

13

that I would not hesitate to sue him; I should judge that I frightened him sufficiently."

His eyes, for the first time, turned toward Van der Valk with something alive behind them. A shade of warmth colored his voice when he again began speaking.

"I am very fond of my wife. If I looked into this scrap of malice any further, it was to insure that I would be able to protect her from the consequences of any indiscreet word or impulse. The man Cabestan, I found, lived in a sort of apartment in the attic of a house occupied by a doctor that my wife has indeed consulted. I have consulted him myself. He is an excellent doctor, skillful and sensitive. He is, I believe, well known in his profession as unorthodox, possibly, in his methods, but as a man who cures his patients. I had, in short, no reason whatever to wish him ill or to suspect him of ill. I concluded that the whole tale was a piece of malicious invention. For I had inquiries made about this Cabestan. He has lost his reputation —had, I should say. He drank too much, was reduced to all sorts of shifts to make ends meet. Then I learned it accidentally while glancing at the newspapers; it was the usual three-line item in a column of fatal accidents—the man had died suddenly, the cause of death, seemingly, a trifle obscure. It held my attention. I have not much experience of blackmailers"—the words were spoken quite without irony— "but it did engage my thought that if such a one had a stronger hold on someone than that which this man had upon me, and if he tried to exert pressure upon a person such as myself with a certain public life, he would then run a risk of an attack. With your experi-

14

ence, you will know how much weight to give to this point. I come to the kernel of my tale.

"Only a day or two after I read about the death, my wife went to see this doctor. She made no secret of it; I asked her indifferently where she was going and she answered freely that she had been told to go for a checkup. It was a small point but it was the second small coincidence to catch my attention, and for the first time I took the whole matter seriously. I am not going to tell you how I came to feel certain of the truth but I will tell you this. There are things that one may have cause to tell a doctor, particularly a neurologist. My wife is a young healthy woman with a considerable need for emotional life. I do not, in fact, give her enough interest or amusement. The story has truth. With reluctance I have come to believe that this odious Cabestan had in some way guessed at a fact.

"I do not believe that there is any passion involved, although I am not, perhaps, a very good judge. Under the influence of passion, I can understand that a man might do things he would not ordinarily do. Cabestan, however, was not assaulted, or struck, as I understand. You may, of course, disregard my beliefs, but I have a feeling that the man was murdered, in some manner that a doctor might choose, in order to keep the association with my wife from reaching any ears.

"If that is so, you might ask why I should intervene, since it is obviously in my interest to keep silent. It has not been easy. I choose to disregard my wife's actions—I do not believe her guilty of any complicity in this death. I realize what the consequences will be if any such complicity should be discovered. I have still found myself forced to speak. In the position I occupy, in the function that I fill, with its many bearings on public life—you realize that I am frequently called upon to give decisions regarding municipal and even state projects—I have sometimes had to decide whether or not I might be contributing to dishonesty, even corruption. I have sometimes closed my eyes and remained certain that I was bringing a benefit to some people who needed it even if some rogues enriched themselves along the way. But a banker, Mr. van der Valk, cannot, by the same law and in the same breath, give way to a dishonest silence regarding a crime. As an officer of law under oath, you will understand that. I might add that a doctor has also a professional oath."

"It is not, in fact, going to be exactly easy for any one of the three of us," said Van der Valk abruptly. Suddenly he could not stand all this another minute; he opened the auto door and stepped thankfully out into fresh air. "You have to understand, Mr. Merckel, that you have given this matter long thought, as you tell me," he added more calmly. "Before I can tell what can or will be done in the light of all this, I have to do some serious thinking myself. Just tell me where I can get in touch with you."

He stood vaguely in the middle of the pavement with tourists bumping into him as they walked along staring vacantly up the New Side Voorburgwal. He gave a loud sigh, as though he had been very thirsty and had drunk a whole glass of cold beer in one breath, and a slovenly woman dragging in her garbage pail stared at him, recognized him, and gave a squawking cackle of laughter.

"Whatsamatter, Smiler—in love?"

16

He hadn't even the heart to look at her.

"Stuck-up, these days," she remarked, slamming the door after herself and her garbage pail indignantly.

2

The morning, and most of the afternoon, since really the disposal of the pornographic-magazines man was child's play, he spent finding out all he could about the death of one Cabestan, together with any information he could pick up about Mr. Carl Merckel, managing director of Lutz Brothers, merchant bankers, and Dr. Hubert van der Post, neurologist, specialist in short-wave and other electrical treatments. There wasn't much. The doctor who had been called to look at Cabestan—a young G.P. who often did police work in the precinct but was not an official police surgeon—had signed a death certificate indicating heart failure as cause of death, and had scribbled in a few pointers that had struck him as obviously explanatory. Cabestan was a chronic drinker, if not actually alcoholic in the clinical sense, had suffered from bronchial trouble, and had lived in a flat up three long steep flights of stairs. No elevator, and anything heavy, like a butane-gas cylinder, had to be carried up those three flights. A sudden exertion, suggested the doctor on the telephone, a shortage of breath, a circulatory and respiratory system weakened by abusive use of alcohol . . . Nobody had dreamed of questioning this death. Cabestan had been found dressed, on the floor, a good thirty-six hours after death, by some acquaintance who had wondered why he was nowhere to be seen, had been bothered at getting no answer to rapping on the door, and had finally warned the landlord—Dr. Hubert van der Post, who lived in the house. . . .

No, not the Doctor, who had been busy with patients. The secretary, said a brief police report, had found a spare key kept in case of fire—for the attic flat had a totally separate street door—and had given it to the policeman, had stated that the two households had had nothing to do with each other, that she barely knew Cabestan, who had been the tenant since the time of the last owner, and that he was an untroublesome person who paid his rent regularly.

Dr. Post, seen briefly at lunchtime, had been courteous and concerned, had confirmed that he hardly knew his tenant, and had suggested calling the bank that paid the rent.

The bank had equally little to say. It had handled Cabestan for thirty years. He had made a fortune in his day, but had for ten years now gone through lean times. Yes, they had received odd irregular payments. They always had; it was normal that an artist earned his living in irregular lump sums. There was very little in the account at the time of death. His executor was a younger brother in the provinces, a small-town builder-contractor, who had seen nothing of his brother in twenty years; neither their paths nor their interests had ever coincided.

No breath of scandal had ever touched either the banker or the Doctor. Plenty was known about the public lives of both; little about the private lives of either. The Doctor had been married, first marriage on both sides, childless. He had a degree from Amsterdam, another from Edinburgh, had authored various postgraduate studies and papers, but wasn't a member of any learned societies, nor did he hold any defined consultant or hospital posts. Purely private practice, slightly nonconformist in methods, extensive connection with society patients, regarded as very skillful and able.

The banker had been married and was likewise childless; in his case, there were second marriages on both sides—first wife a Jewess, died in Canada in exile during war years. Remarried to attractive and elegant young widow of editor of lively provincial daily paper; editor shot by Germans as resistance worker in 1944. The widow was left with one daughter at the age of twenty-two. Remarried at thirty when working as secretary to banking colleague. There had never been the slightest sign of malaise in this marriage.

Van der Valk, liking it all less and less, was unpleasant the whole afternoon to everyone he met, and was even rude about the supper he got that evening from his wife, for no reason at all; it was spaghetti, which he always enjoyed.

The clouds had broken up and vanished; the weather forecast was for a prolonged period of settled summer weather, warm and clear. A perfect evening. Arlette looked at her husband and decided resignedly that it was no use expecting any help with the dishes. The two boys, who had been outside since coming home from school, tried to sneak out again, and she had a struggle getting them to go to their room to do their homework. A summer evening is no great joy to children at the lyceum; never does the homework sit on the stomach with a more leaden weight.

19

Ordinarily, Van der Valk would simply have told them to stop their nonsense, but now he disregarded the squabble altogether. He had passed into his trance. He pushed two potted plants to one side, sat on the window sill, lit a cigar, and stared heavily at the traffic below. He thought best while leaning out of windows gazing at autos, bicycles, pedestrians. It was as though his thoughts reached the widest scope only in this detached yet close contact with people.

He stared at a little pretty German auto, brand new, painted an obnoxious color. He considered the color carefully. It is that, he decided, of cheap tinned tomato soup, found only in the nastiest restaurants and the laziest homes. It is a small auto, he thought, produced in huge numbers, in a limited range of colors; *ergo,* the Germans have no sense of color. If they had, they would not make these things in such evidently great numbers. He was disgusted when, by one of those coincidences that are a corrective to pride and faulty deduction, a larger, much more expensive auto of a renowned French make came sailing down the street a moment later—painted the identical nauseating shade.

There were two main problems; he had to find a tactic to match both. First, no policeman in his senses would take this wasp's nest seriously. Officially, there were too many toes to trip over, and such sensitive toes. . . . Not the remotest chance of ever finding out the truth. Bound up with this was problem 2. No policeman in his senses would launch himself into an investigation where Heer Merckel held him in leading strings. Lay off my wife and family; lay off me. Otherwise—just remember, will you, who my friends are! It wasn't that the man was dishonest. But his mentality was so tortuous that he could ask—he had asked—for an investigation into an affair he suspected was criminal, since his delicate moral nostrils were offended by it. He could say, nobly, that his wife's possible involvement made no difference to his conscience. But if that investigation started pressing on his private life, woe to the investigator. To this mentality, the two states of mind were quite compatible. Morality was maintained.

Even if Van der Valk pushed through into an official inquiry, even if Mr. Samson authorized it—which, of course, he wouldn't—one tiny false step and it would be his, Van der Valk's, neck. It couldn't be any other way, with both the banker and the Doctor ready with the hatchet.

Was there any way out? Suppose, just suppose . . . that he never made any official inquiry at all, that he operated entirely alone, not only without official help, cognizance, or support but in direct contradiction to all police regulations. Van der Valk in the romantic, intoxicating, ridiculous role of private eye. Philip van der Marlowe.

A highly ludicrous notion, attributable to his overready imagination, which many superior officers had frequently told him was his worst enemy. But tempting, considered purely as a tactic. He would have to behave, if he was going to find anything out, in an unethical way. Samson mustn't know—anyway not till later. Because if he found his subordinate doing anything unethical, he would crucify the clown.

Merckel couldn't make a complaint, because a complaint could only apply to an official action. Merckel had wanted to stay anonymous; very well, Van der Valk would simply deny that he had ever heard of Merckel, and the complaint would boil down to lack of action taken on an anonymous letter that was in itself unjustifiable. Merckel, having made no official approach, could make no official complaint.

Van der Valk found himself testing his theory in an imaginary conversation with Mr. Samson:

"Damned complicated cock-and-bull story." That was Samson.

"You can say that again." Van der Valk, playing his little part.

"Now, why does this banker come secretly to us in this extraordinary way, when if he's not satisfied he has only to call one of his pals and ask for his name to be kept out of it?" Samson asks.

"Maybe he has guilt feelings," Van der Valk replies.

"Maybe he did it himself and wonders whether we have any queries. He was being blackmailed. He has no evidence that the Doctor was. His tale is odd. He explains his certainty that his wife was playing games with the Doctor, but not his certainty that the Doctor killed this Cabestan—what a name!" says Samson.

"But if Cabestan had anything on the wife, he had it on the Doctor, too. He would put the screw on both together," Van der Valk says.

"Suppose his evidence of misbehavior—what a phrase!—was not conclusive. Cabestan's, I mean. He thinks a doctor likelier to hit back, to make an accusation of slander. He concentrates on the woman, thinking her husband is in a position where he would be extremely adverse to that kind of publicity. She tells her husband, knowing he is not jealous. Husband knocks off this Cabestan, then gets scared a post-mortem would show violence. Tells us, making accusations about the Doctor, hinting at things he guesses we'll find out anyway. Hmm?"

"The medical report was superficial, didn't show a damn thing. The fellow was in poor health—heart failure quite likely and natural. I looked it up this morning," Van der Valk says.

"I'm not applying for any goddam exhumation orders on this gossip. You've looked up the Doctor?" asks Samson.

"He's well known. Nothing whatever shady. Society practice. Neurologist. Good at curing sleeping-pill addiction—that kind of thing. Nothing fishy at all—properly qualified and everything," says Van der Valk.

"I see. You told this Merckel, I hope, that we were not bound to take any action at all, whoever he is and whoever his friends are?" Samson asks.

"Of course. Odd thing—he knows the Doctor himself—got cured of some obscure trouble. He genuinely believes in a murder—has no real malice against the Doctor at all." Van der Valk shakes his head.

"We can't take any official action. Much too tricky a setup. Perhaps—just barely possible—you might try unofficially to find out more about this Doctor. But the breath of a complaint and I disown you. Get it?"

"I get it."

"This Merckel, quite plainly, has not told all he knows."

"Exactly the impression I got," Van der Valk says.

"You just might shake something loose—even with no official standing whatever. You're supposed to have some brains somewhere, aren't you?"

This imaginary conversation was, Van der Valk thought, quite impossible. Samson, once he knew the situation, would order Van der Valk or anybody else categorically to lay off. But there was one important thing to know about the old man. He could and did close his eyes to all sorts of irregularities and enormities provided he knew nothing about them officially. Out of his long experience, he knew that the ever-increasing mass of regulations and the bristling juridical double talk strangled all initiative and reduced a cautious police officer too often to impotence. He knew that his subordinates, to get results, were often forced to break rules. In order to avoid issuing an official ukase, he wished never to be officially told. If any complaint arrived, he would stand up for his squad, stubbornly, effectively.

Now, Kan always went by the book. Rigidly, scrupulously, and insisting on knowing everything. But Kan was away. And the old boy didn't care what you did as long as you got results. You were on your own. If you won he gave you full credit. But if you lost—got caught doing something not just outside the borderline of the rules but something downright unethical—he would unhesitatingly throw you to the wolves.

A hell of a gamble, this.

Van der Valk liked his tactical notion, though. He would go and have a crack at the Doctor. He'd get in pretending to be a patient, perhaps. The man would be—assuming that there was anything he was guilty of at all—badly shaken at the appearance of what could only be police, or another blackmailer just after he had got rid of the first. And if he wasn't guilty of anything at all? Well, then, one would need to withdraw very skillfully indeed, because one was in a bad fix.

But Van der Valk felt strongly that there was something about this Doctor that would dislike the notion of daylight. Also there had been something about Heer Merckel that had been oddly convincing.

3

A successful fashionable doctor, thought Van der Valk vaguely, is likely to be a rigid, arid person, living in an expensive featureless house surrounded by his precious "standing." But this one was, at the very first glance, more interesting, showing, even on the extreme outside, marks of personality.

Take his house, now. An old-fashioned house on a street that was no longer fashionable—heavy houses in an ugly style from the epoch of the Kaiser's heyday, around 1910, perhaps. But ugliness was redeemed from the start by the trees in front, lindens in full foliage, allowed to reach their full proportions—a rarity in Amsterdam as in all Dutch towns, where the municipality's tidiness neurosis becomes, faced with anything as messy and unhygienic as a tree, very nearly psychotic. The explanation seemed to be that the pavement here was, for Amsterdam, unusually wide, and even for Amsterdam unusually dusty.

The neighborhood seemed dingy for a fashionable doctor, and the doctors that remained between import-export agencies, South American consulates, and sales offices for German factories had a faintly obscurantist sound, judging by the brass plates. Gerontologist, otolaryngo— Damn it, he thought, why not just say ear, nose, and throat? The large, simple, well-polished brass plate that said "H. v. d. Post, Neurologist. By appointment only" was matched by another that said, politely, "Please note that this entrance is for patients ONLY. ALL other callers or inquiries at Wozzeckstr. 14."

So. A mews entrance; that was interesting. The curtains looked rich and velvety; the house was carefully painted. What was slightly odd about it? Of course—the extra street door at the corner, added with no regard for the architectural balance. That was where this Cabestan had lived, up in the attic.

Well—now or never. If he was a policeman, he had been instructed to go around to the back with his hat in his hand. If he was a patient, he might very probably be out of a job next week. Van der Marlowe crossed his palm with silver, gazed at the new moon through glass, and walked up the short gravel path. The door to the practice was a heavy old affair with carved panels. Ordinarily these doors open, but this one resisted his efforts to turn the handle. He rang, and a voice answered at once over a speaker concealed behind a rococo wrought-iron grille. The quiet voice of a middle-aged woman.

"May I know who you are, please?"

"My name is Van der Valk, but you don't know me."

"You wish to consult the Doctor?"

"Yes." What else could one say to an intercom?

"Would you be so good as to come straight up the stairs you will see in the hallway and into the room marked 'Secretary'? Thank you."

The door buzzed and clicked. A neat notice at eye level said, "Please close it behind you." Hat rack; he hung his hat, could always come back later to hang himself. Hall furniture, fairly sumptuous, colorless. Stairs, doors on a landing. At the end a curtained portière, the living quarters. He walked obediently into "Secretary," which was a small neat office, bright with clear colors and flowers. A thin, light woman, with blued hair, rimless octagonal glasses, and an effaced green woolly frock sat at the desk.

"Mr. van der Valk? I am Miss Maas. Do please sit down. What time of day do you prefer for an appointment?"

"I would very much like to see the Doctor today if at all possible."

She smiled professionally. "That is usually very difficult, but as it happens I do have a cancellation this morning. But I will have to ask you to wait half an hour. Would you prefer to come back? Will that suit?"

"Perfectly." Her smile approved of him beamingly for not being difficult.

"Just give your name at the speaker."

He had time for a stroll into the Wozzeckstraat. It was a lane sandwiched between two rows of noble-looking houses that had gardens. There were high walls, garages, sheds where obscure little businesses were carried on. An "interior decorator," a coppersmith, a hand weaver, a window cleaner—plebeian amidst the artists but certainly with four times their income. The back of the Doctor's house was a garage with a flat above it—chauffeur doubtless, possibly doubling as gardener, and wife as concierge, for there was another brass plate. "For all messages, goods delivered, offers, or collections. H. v. d. Post." In the lane stood a cherry-red Alfa Romeo town car with the entwined snake at the windshield corner. Again—a bit of an individual auto for a doctor. Still . . . He walked on as far as the water, where he stood gazing, rattling small change in his trouser pocket.

When he got back, the secretary handed him an orange form. He gave his own home address, his profession as Businessman.

"Have you been recommended to come here by any other doctor? You just came on your own— I see," brightly still. "And have you a state insurance number, or is yours private? Thank you so much. I'll be calling you within five minutes, probably."

Well, there he was. A patient, and he hadn't been told to go to the back door. Would the Doctor send a bill for professional services to the police department? Ha. Van der Valk felt buoyant, he felt lucky. He was confident, now that he was in, that he wouldn't get flung out on his ear. The intercom clicked above his head and the bright soft voice addressed him.

"Mr. van der Valk, would you be so kind as to take the door on your left at the bottom of the stairs? Doctor van der Post is ready for you." The organization here is pretty good, he thought on his way down; they don't have a heap of people sitting staring at each other—and that fact, no doubt, is reflected in the bills patients get presented with.

28

4

He had no time to absorb the surroundings that first
visit. It was later that he discovered afresh innumerable
details of the figure, its background, its frame, and
began to fit them in, for they were all broken up and
jumbled by the jigsaw—the strain induced and the
boldness needed. Carrying through with this confidence trick, this quite brazen piece of imposture, had
not been at all easy. When he left the house, he was
stunned with nervous fatigue and with a confused
heap of uncoordinated impressions. He stood blinking
at the traffic flowing along the main road, a hundred
yards down from the house with the lindens. He did
not know quite what to do; it was late for going back
to an office where there was, he hoped, nothing for
him to do but catch up on some neglected paper work,
and it was too early to go home. Besides, the smell of
dinner cooking, of his house, of his wife's skin when
he kissed her, the whole feeling of home—no no, that
would all destroy the very picture he was trying to
paint, the coloring he was trying to pin down. He
needed something to do, something small and unimportant, that would be symbolic of what, to him,
promised to become a particularly delicate and risky
piece of work.

He walked with heavy steps into a stationer's,
where he bought three cardboard folders. A little farther was a café, where he sat down deliberately to examine his purchase. Not feeling at all in need of
alcohol, he ordered a black-currant juice. There was a
green folder, a sort of insipid Nile green, and a beige

one; he shoved these to the back of his briefcase. A gray one seemed to him the most suitable. He fished for a ball-point and lettered it, in neat capitals, "C.M.P." Cabestan-Merckel-Post, Canadian Mineral Prospectors, Consolidated Madagascan Potash.

There was certainly a connection. That this Doctor had killed Cabestan was not impossible. That he played games with the more sympathetic of his women patients was, perhaps, even probable. Because, thought Van der Valk, meditating over his black-currant juice and his scribbling pad, he rather believed that Dr. Post knew why he had come, even if Van der Valk had not known himself. Oh, yes, he could fly balloons about the coincidental death of a seedy painter who had happened to live in the attic up above, but there was not proof enough to condemn a cockroach on, and Post knew that. Did he know that just because he was a doctor, with the professional knowledge of a man who has at some time taken a course in forensic medicine, or was it the cynicism of a man laughing at the amazing naïveté and stupidity of the police? Van der Valk didn't know. That attitude of amused indifference.

Had he gone about this the right way? But once in a false position—in a situation where any position would be false—it was hard to see how else he could have done it. He could have retreated promptly into his official identity and said the words out of the book, upon which the Doctor—any doctor, knowing a little about the world—would have challenged him. There was no evidence of any weight at all, and the impudent bluff would have been called.

Van der Valk had followed, perhaps, that instinct

that made him a dangerous policeman and that sometimes so alarmed his superiors: his instinct for fitting his approach toward a problem to the nature of the problem. In a false position a false game. He had pretended, for a moment, to be a patient, and had then embarked on a transparent fiction that these suspicions were really delusions to be discussed in confidence—even that he was presenting unusual symptoms to a doctor's scrutiny for analysis and judgment. He was asking for a diagnosis; that was it.

"You know," Post had said, with his constant smile, "this is really a good example of what the books call a systematized fantasy, don't you agree?" He had a twenty-two-carat professional manner, the exact blend of interested sympathy and studied objectivity. But he was no cheap smoothy, like the man inviting you to sign the hire-purchase agreement.

"You are, by your account, a police officer, with a highly improbable tale; you are aware how improbable it must sound, and that, not unnaturally, makes you uneasy. So you explain your presence in my house with the remark that since you have received an accusation relating to me, and since I am also a doctor, you feel that the simplest way of handling your unease is to pretend informality, coming and asking what I think of it all, inviting, as it were, my discreet cooperation. Have I understood your somewhat confused remarks?"

"Very well. Wouldn't you agree that it was not only the simplest way but the right method? My unease—perfectly true—exists because the facts as I know them lie outside my understanding. Since you are a neurologist, I call you into consultation."

Van der Valk added his own smile to Post's.

"Do I even know you are a real policeman?"

Van der Valk passed his identity card across the desk.

"Most remarkable. Well, apart from repeating the obvious—that your informant, since I take it there is an informant, needs medical treatment that I am probably not competent to exercise—I cannot see how I can help. I could even complain to the police department that my time was being wasted by an officer highly enough placed to know better, since you have no interrogatory commission or official standing."

This was unpleasantly slippery; Van der Valk hurried off the ice. "Come," he said, in the pleasant tone the other used, with the same perpetual smile, the same detached amusement. "Come, now, you wouldn't do that. If you are asked to examine a person—I won't say a patient, because you are convinced, let us say, that there is nothing whatever wrong with him—you would still do so. Discreetly, dispassionately. You would not tell this man that he was either ill or well. First, quietly, you would try to find out. Am I not right? Of course I'm right. Naturally you agree. I am a police officer. Instead of complaining that I have no commission or mandate—a thing for which there is no call or need—be glad that I don't arrive on your doorstep with a flourish, telling your secretary who or what I am, giving rise to scandal and innuendo. You may have something in your life you would not wish the police to investigate. Even little things can be very damaging to a professional man." A remark, he thought with pleasure, that could not have tripped more smoothly off the lips of the most accomplished blackmailer.

It was the smile, and the fastidious fingers, that stayed with him most after that first meeting with Dr. Hubert van der Post. The smile was warm and charming, but it was Olympian. He found everything amusing because it was seen from a great height of superiority. He was set so far apart from the ruck, so far above the roughened fingers, broken nails, grimy knuckles, that he could see little but comedy in agitated sweaty little men like Van der Valk. Perhaps it was less a question of vanity than a sense of humility that was missing from his character. A humiliation would be the worst blow, possibly, that anyone could give him.

Everything about him, too—his clothes, his desk, his room. Van der Valk tried to think of adjectives to fit. Delicate, exact, in exquisite taste, purified of all vulgarity. Masculine, certainly. But a little too poised, a scrap too exquisite. Would he be inclined to see all sadness, all worry, as merely tiny, ludicrous incidents that could and would never touch, bother, irritate, penetrate this room?

5

Mr. Samson seemed to have found a solution to Cross-Eyed Janus, unless he had simply given it up. He showed no sign of being in either a good humor or a bad one, but then he never did. He was reading a pornographic magazine, part of the loot from the unfortunate gentleman whose auto had fallen in the canal. It could not have been interesting, because he put it down quickly when Van der Valk came in to make his report.

"Well, now, how's your little affair?"

Van der Valk told about the cautious games with taxis around the Javakade and the remarks made by Heer Merckel, at which Mr. Samson began pulling faces.

"Another one with a puritan conscience, shoveling it all on top of us. Could just as easily have knocked off this Capstan—or whatever his name is—himself, assuming anybody ever did knock him off—huh?"

"Nothing to show he didn't. I was fed up, I can tell you," Van der Valk said.

"Not surprised, though, I hope. You wait till you've been in this department as long as I have. There isn't one in ten of this type that has any basis in fact. They feel bothered by something they've got involved in that seems a scrap dirtier than their usual lives, and they turn it around in their minds till they reach a completely illogical certainty that a crime has been committed. I've seen dozens of them. They come racing in to tell us about it and then they feel much better. Leaving me to pull the plug when they're quite finished. As for concrete evidence, that doesn't enter their scheme of things. Morality is what bothers them. If we had less morality, we might have more justice. Want a dirty book? It's bloody dull." Mr. Samson was in a good mood, after all. Van der Valk decided to admit that he had thought there was a little more to Mr. Merckel than a suburban housewife with a guilty conscience.

"You thinking of doing anything about this Doctor?" Samson said. "There isn't anything you can do—

34

I read that medical report. No positive indication of any interference with natural processes, and without that we can't move. This Merckel of yours isn't worth a burned match."

"I saw the Doctor, though."

"You mean without getting chucked out?" Samson asked.

"I didn't show my card. His secretary took me for a patient and just let me in without asking. There I was, sitting in the chair."

The Commissaris pushed his glasses down and stared over them. "Look, boy, if this Doctor raises a stink, I'm the one on the block."

"He won't complain. Complaining would make his fingers dirty. He's far above such things. He treated it all as though it were just funny. I think, too, he'd be scared. He gave me a lot of time. There's something there he wouldn't want to come out."

"You mean you think he does amuse himself with the women patients?"

"He amuses himself with everything."

"How do you know that?" Samson asked.

"How does one ever know anything? He amused himself with me. It struck me afterward. You see, I went in there and told him that I had unsupported information and that I had to look into it, blah blah, and chose to come and talk it over discreetly, unofficially —to cover myself, of course. Well. He took this up, began to weave a comic analogy. It was funny. I was a neurotic patient, come to him with fantasies, which he then has to treat. It tickled him. I'm his patient; he is going to diagnose the nature of my delusions. I liked that. I started trying to diagnose him. There's something out-of-the-ordinary about him."

Mr. Samson put his elbows on the table and stared at his subordinate with a square, wooden expression. "Go on," he said, in an ominous voice.

"I had my foot in the door, I thought, and by pure luck, since I was expecting clam-up and to be told 'The door is over there.' So I said to him, 'Now that I'm your patient, I'll be coming again for consultation —treatment, too, perhaps.' I thought he'd tell me off. He just grinned and said, "Perhaps your delusions will be interesting enough to warrant my continuing this file.' The secretary had filled out one of those cardboard files with my name and age—that crap. I knew he was scared then. He wants to keep in touch, to hear if I say anything, to try and know what I think. There must be something there."

"Yes," agreed the old man.

"So I went out and bought myself a cardboard folder, too. And wrote his goddam name on it." Van der Valk finished, and realized that he had spoken with an emphasis that had something approaching fury in it. Old Samson nearly grinned.

"All right, my boy. Just bear one thing in mind. If this chap is playing with you, he doesn't need to make a complaint. I see what's in your mind. You think that because you've made no formal move, he can't make a formal complaint to old Kaiser Franz Joseph upstairs. True, but I looked up this Doctor of yours. He says one quiet word to some high pooha and your days in this department are over. He's married to a whole family of magistrates—friends everywhere and

Lord knows whom he may have in his pocket. Grateful ex-patients, quite probably including the Minister of Justice. I won't be able to save you."

It was a long speech. Van der Valk realized that if the old man didn't approve of what he had done, there would have been just a grunt, if that.

"If every time we broke a rule we stopped to think what would happen if we got the sack, how many things would we miss?" Van der Valk said. "Would we ever get Janus, for example?" It was an impudent remark; the old man went a bit turkey-cocky.

"You bother about this Doctor and leave me to deal with Janus." It was as near a green light as Van der Valk would ever get. As he went out, Mr. Samson threw the pornographic book in the wastepaper basket. The last Van der Valk saw, he was stooping, purple, to fish it out again, having just remembered that the cleaning women would find it.

"How's Father?" said Inspector Scholten, who shared his office and was deep in some administrative rigmarole.

"Reading a dirty book."

"He was on the rampage this morning. Said he wished Kan was back. Minute later he said when he saw Kan, he'd kick him so he'd never dare have piles again."

"Why?" He was obviously expected to ask why.

"Kan sent in a report he'd done at home, saying he'd explored every possibility and there wasn't any legal hold on that Janus character. Old man went fair mataglap. Not my pigeon, thank God."

"Ah." Van der Valk rather thought he understood.

6

A week later. Brilliant weather: August heat over Amsterdam. The mornings were clear and splendid; the afternoons reeled with sun and the pavements danced under temperatures in the nineties. The evenings had a pleasant coolness, but at night the thunder rumbled and the lightning flashed. Sometimes huge spots of rain fell, but always by midnight the charged clouds had passed, and the humidity with them, and the thermometer went down to sixty, and fresh cool air flickered in at bedroom windows.

It was the silly season. Almost everybody was in Spain or Italy. Commissaris Samson had a chalet on a West Frisian island and was away for three weeks. Scholten was camping in a tent somewhere in the south. Kan was back, grumbling; his holiday was not due till September. As for Van der Valk, he had gone on holiday in June. It had rained all the time but he hadn't cared. They had had a cottage on the Loire, belonging to Arlette's brother, who was a specialist in stressed concrete and was busy on a building project down in Toulon—where it was raining, too, much to Arlette's satisfaction. They had been thoroughly lazy, doing little but swim, arguing that that way you didn't get any wetter.

He didn't care; he liked the warm Amsterdam weather, and the quiet. There was not much to do; it was too hot. For the sun was blazing down on Holland, and everybody was grumbling, of course, and walking about as naked as possible, sweaty and uncomfortable, guzzling fizzy lemonade whenever they got the chance. Not him. He was married to a woman who came from the Midi; he knew how to behave in warm weather, and he had his shirt buttoned up and even a jacket on. He sat in the office drinking tea and beaming at Chief Inspector Kan, who looked thoroughly uncomfortable and undignified in his unaccustomed shirt sleeves, fanning himself with the latest *Monthly Supplement to the General Police Standing Orders and Instructions*—a singularly dismal document.

"Lamentable," he was saying. "Lamentable." Kan was rather a one for literature, and when he made out an official report, he always had a dictionary at his elbow, since law, he said, depended on the precise meanings of words. The hunt for the exact word preoccupied him greatly, and not long before he had put "apotheosis" in a report, causing Mr. Samson to take his glasses off and say with awful quiet, "There are times, Chief Inspector, when I should like to take a fast run of about a hundred yards at you doing up your shoelace." Kan, who was one of the new university-degree career policemen, despised Samson, and told the inspectors sometimes that the old man "was not oriented to modern methods."

Still, Kan was handy in many ways. Van der Valk thought him a sharp-nosed little twerp, a pedantic fusspot, and a scared baby-sitter, but could not deny that he knew his law backward, and, apparently, the entire history and background of every company director in Holland. He was very smart when it came to economics—and most criminal work in Holland is a question of economics—but he didn't like murders, and Samson, the old-fashioned type of policeman who had learned his work on the streets, never gave him work of that kind. As a consequence, he interfered very little with Van der Valk. This job now—the C.M.P. file. He would have had a fit if he had known the things his nominal subordinate was thinking up, but the innocent had not noticed that his brains were being picked.

"Well, now," Kan was saying, "you know that I have a lot of doctor friends. I looked up your man pretty carefully. Very brilliant student, came from a good family. There was an uncle on the mother's side who was Governor General of the East Indies. People of standing. I agree, of course, that those days are gone, but it still counts, you know. You'd be surprised, Van der Valk, but then you know nothing about this class of person. His wife's family carries a lot of weight, too. An uncle of hers was Queen's Commissioner for one of the eastern provinces; it's slipped my mind now exactly which. It'll come back to me.

"Her father was only a canton magistrate, but there is a brother who is a Substitute Officer of Justice, been transferred recently to Utrecht—getting near the top, my lad," with admiration. "And there is a cousin who is an Advocate to the Court of Appeal—most distinguished family. I would say that it was the marriage more than the man himself that made him. His reputation's sound, of course, but there's something, from what I hear— He's clever enough but lacking fiber, if you understand me. He's brilliant, yes, but a thought lightweight, a scrap too unusual, dabbles a bit in chimerical theories. I'd almost go as far as to say that he's never been quite altogether accepted by the very top members of the profession."

Kan was well launched on just the sort of thing that pleased him: his famous accurate précis—it could not be called a thumbnail sketch—of the character and attainments of someone in public life.

"There's been a certain amount of comment on the marriage, too, I hear. She's a splendid woman, thoroughly intelligent, broad intellectual interests, knowing what is expected of her position. Naturally, one makes a remark like this guardedly, but it has been said that people felt she'd rather thrown herself away. A man of remarkable promise, who hadn't quite fulfilled the hopes people had of him."

"Thanks very much," said Van der Valk, poker-faced busily drawing little imps of malice with vicious horns and curly spiky tails in the margin of his scribbling pad. "That's a big help."

"You don't need the warning of course," Kan went on generously, "but bear in mind, won't you, that people would be very slow to accept the idea of his being in any way dubious, don't you know? Even if it were only for her sake. He himself, I rather think, hasn't very many friends; I mean close friends. A bit stand-offish, prickly, not really a very good mixer, and of course that's so important." He brooded, while Van der Valk thought that if there were a modern version of Samuel Smiles' *Self-Help*, or a *Guide for the Rising Young Executive*, they could get Kan to write the Foreword to the Dutch edition.

"But I wouldn't want to give you an unbalanced picture; he has a very wealthy and important circle of patients, and there's no doubt at all of his success or his talent. Just that he doesn't quite belong, you know, in the milieu where it really counts. Still, of course, you remember the sort of experience we had in that disgraceful affair of the one who was picked up for drunk driving. They all close the ranks—you'd never get one of them to come into court and say it outright."

"More or less like Janus," Van der Valk said naughtily.

"Good heavens, man, there's no comparison."

"Can't see much difference."

"There are still things you have to learn," Kan said snubbingly.

"You, too," amiably. "Like staying away from that horse-piss lemonade on a day like this." Chief Inspector Kan opened his mouth as soon as he had thought of a suitable phrase, but Van der Valk was out of the door by then.

7

It had developed rapidly enough into the situation no policeman sees with any enthusiasm—a conviction, virtually a certainty, that a man is guilty of a legally punishable action, without any evidence of anything. Van der Valk had made no written reports; Mr. Samson, he knew, would not want them. No jurist would glance twice at what he had, even if Merckel stood up and said all he knew, which nobody would want him to. Van der Valk felt certain he had been safe in agreeing to leave the banker out of it, since if he ever got anywhere with this, it would be on the strength of his own scheme, aided by nothing but his own tactics.

Those tactics could only be to exploit the odd acceptance Dr. van der Post had shown to his challenge. Peculiar. The man could so easily have hidden behind his official image. Everything he did and everything he said to a patient was confidential. No policeman had a right even to set foot in his house unless he was sent by an official order.

Van der Valk had gone back to chance his luck. He would try a throw of laughable audacity, because if it didn't work there was nothing to do but go home, forget all about Dr. Hubert van der Post, and six months later advise Heer Carl Merckel that we regret we do not see our way at present to granting your application for a loan. It was this course that he was prepared for after listening to Chief Inspector Kan, and anybody else who could tell him anything about doctors.

He had rung up the Doctor's secretary again and asked for another appointment, wondering what he would hear, since a brush-off would be so simple. Had she not been warned that he was unbalanced, or a hypochondriac—or a blackmailer? She would have accepted any explanation, and stalled him politely. "The Doctor feels unable to help you, I'm afraid." Very cool and courteous.

But no. She had heard him say his piece, and had given him an appointment without the slightest hindrance. And when he had walked again into that consulting room, he had been received almost as a guest. It had been—now, yes, embarrassing. That was the only word; it was almost as though the Doctor wished tacitly to admit. Admit what? Why? Bravado? Sarcasm, knowing that the policeman would never find proof? None of the explanations was satisfying.

It was a fine room, originally the drawing room in

the Kaiser's time, when things were done in a big, solid way. Generous windows, with dark-ripe apricot-colored velvet curtains. The olive-green wall-to-wall velvety expensive carpet. Plenty of bookshelves, a couple of decorative pictures. All of it far more front than a doctor will ordinarily present, even an expensive specialist. Outside the windows, the lindens made a luxuriant pattern of sunlight-dappled green against the ivory slats of the Venetian blinds. A big room, and a desk to match, placed diagonally in the corner by the windows. Long fine hands lay on the desk. They looked very relaxed; they played a little with a simple square crystal ash tray, but they did not fiddle. A fountain pen lay on the blotter, with his "file" beside it. The telephone, the desk calendar, the other functional objects, were all cleared away on a swinging typewriter table to one side.

There was a chair opposite; it looked like a comfortable chair, at that. Van der Valk had sat on it the last time but he didn't remember. The thin, neat, upright man in a very well-cut formal suit had that professional but certainly attractive smile around the eyes and the wide thin mouth, just as before, and the hand in the shantung cuff pointed at the sofa.

"People often find that comfortable." A long sofa, with a severe oblong coffee table in front of it. A very good simple vase, to match the ash tray—Vosges crystal—with snapdragons in it today. Van der Valk liked all these things very much. Last time he had been too close to his antagonist, and had not had a chance to study the surroundings. He could survey better from the sofa. Had the Doctor thought of that? Was he deliberately being allowed to sit here, lower, farther back, with a perspective on the room?

This furniture was modern. Over there, though, between the doors behind him, was a console table so mannered, so delicate, that he felt sure it was a faithful copy of some piece by a court ebonist of Louis Quinze. Really, Mme. de Pompadour would not have found this room ugly, and he felt immediately that this beauty, this elegance, was important to the man who sat there at the desk. The elegance was not exclusively feminine, but it was a room where a woman would immediately feel at home, at ease, ready to confide, to blossom. Quite a remarkable notion I have there, thought Van der Valk, making chitchat with the man at the desk.

The man is sure of himself, he thought, absolutely smooth, his self-command unusually well suited to his features, his actions. And yet there is anxiety there. But it was not a simple guessing game, for this was a complicated, sophisticated person. Van der Valk shook his head to get rid of an unpleasant sensation of being trapped in cobwebs, suddenly decided to get up and walk about, and did so, rather to his own surprise, wondering what instinct had told him to yield openly to a feeling of inadequacy.

Post's face, courteous, intelligent, good-humored, smiled at him amusedly. "You plainly do not expect to get help from me. But you hope, as plainly, to find that I can give you relief from the fears and distortions that press upon you. You are feeling harassed. By all means, walk about if it helps you."

Van der Valk had to exert a great deal of his own self-command not to get swept off his feet by a sudden red tide of fury. Now, damn the fellow's bloody cheek! He thought deliberately of standing on a beach, chest-high in water, at the moment a big roller breaks. One wrestles to stay upright, forcing one's feet to stay buried in the shifting, swirling sand against the undertow. As the wave goes back, all the sand is sucked away behind one's heels, and one nearly loses all balance afresh and sits ignominiously in the surf.

"I do walk about. It does help me." Isn't there a kind of wrestling, he thought vaguely, where by pretending to give in you reach a winning position? Or is there a better analogy in a chess sacrifice? Now, that is characteristic of my poor muddled brain; I have really very little idea how to stop myself from looking ridiculous. I have no footing at all. By being friendly and pleasant and ever so cooperative, he had lured me on; I thought he was opening the door for me, and so he was, to watch me fall into the pit dug inside and laugh his head off—and all I can think of is chess, a subject on which my level is roughly that of an averagely bright elementary-school child.

The only advantage he possessed, he thought while staring at a shelf of unhelpful literature, was a kind of vague moral force. The man was expecting an ordinary police reaction; he had to find an extraordinary reply.

He had reached the door to the back when Post made the expected remark.

"I need hardly say, my friend, that those doors lead to my examination rooms, where I do not allow you to wander about unsupervised—nor without permission I do not, naturally, give. Even police inspectors are not allowed upon private property without impressive pieces of paper, which you do not possess simply because, as I have reminded you, you are suffering from delusions."

Van der Valk had found himself suddenly. He turned in the closed doorway, grinning, with his hands in his pockets.

"I have something funny to tell you."

The face behind the desk was so impassive that he knew it was forcing itself, for just a second, to conceal a flicker of uncertainty.

"I see things, oddly enough, just the other way around," Van der Valk said. "I find that the moment I walk into this consulting room our positions are reversed, that the patient here is you and the doctor is myself. Nor do I think you are suffering from delusions. I find you to be suffering from a very banal illness, as banal as nervous fatigue would be to you. An illness upon which I am the specialist. Because dishonesty, you see, is an illness. I don't just mean telling lies, of course. Lies are part of the human whole, and I know from my experience that asking a man to stop telling lies is like giving him an ax and telling him to chop his big toe off. Only a very rare man has the force to do without his lies, since they are an integral part of him. Your illness is more of an infection."

"I must congratulate you on the vivacity of your illustrations," murmured the mask.

"You know what makes people—intelligent, highly trained, very perceptive people, like yourself—commit crimes? Even violent crimes, like murders? I'm not talking about little foibles like sleeping with other people's wives. It is because they are wounded in a

47

deep sensitive part, and it is so painful that their reaction is uncontrollable. Wounded in their mechanism of self-deception, an area too complex for us poor ignorant doctors to follow, mostly."

"May I interrupt?"

"No, you mayn't. Remember your professional training. Let the deluded person run on; listen to him in patience," Van der Valk said.

"By all means." The smile had been dropped; Van der Valk was glad to see that a look of slightly polite boredom had been assumed.

"Now, as a doctor, suppose for a moment that I was carried here into your consulting room with a bullet in my stomach that had penetrated the nerve centers, what treatment would you advise?"

"Surgery, my poor friend; that is what carpenters are for."

"Just so. I am only a carpenter and on that account you despise me, but they have their uses, as you will see. You're coming on nicely now; I'm glad I didn't underestimate your intelligence. Quite soon now you'll be realizing that I'm about to operate on you for a badly infected wound to your self-esteem that without swift treatment is extremely dangerous to your whole life."

There was a silence. Van der Valk supposed that it was the silence of a man collecting his courage rather than his wits. He had, after all, banked upon Post's being an extremely intelligent and sensitive person.

"You are beginning to realize," Van der Valk went on smilingly, "that this, at the moment, is not your consulting room at all. It's mine. And since an examination is plainly necessary to aid our diagnosis, we examine everything—in the examination room." Theatrically he opened the door behind him, turned calmly, and walked in. There was no protest from the desk.

"The pieces of paper that you talk about so irrelevantly"—his voice floated back through the doorway —"are things used and needed by bums with no brains. As one intelligent man, you should be able to recognize another. You have lots of electrical equipment, I see. You ought to be a skillful electrician, or am I guessing?"

"Yes," came Post's quiet ironic voice this time. "But occasionally these devices' most successful use is in impressing the ignorant layman. I believe you have something of the same technique . . . colleague." Van der Valk had to laugh at that.

"Admirable point. Lovely garden you have. Ah, and this is where the confident, relaxed, cooperative patient lies on the couch—very comfortable, too—and gets his ills diagnosed by skillful hands. Your finger tips are probably your chief weapon—am I wrong? The invisible antennae. I'm quite ignorant about your branch of medicine, I'm bound to admit. We specialists are pretty much all the same, though; what do you know, for instance, about the diseases of the lung?"

"Practically nothing," Post said.

"That's our trouble; we just can't keep up with modern science even if we were to spend all day reading the newest literature. My, what a lovely bathroom; it makes me feel unwashed. Another psychological aid, I take it, to the patient's confidence in his recovery— or is it purely for your personal use? I must congratulate you on your taste in material objects. And on a very nice, very well-arranged house. We come out here, no doubt," reappearing suddenly, with a broad beam of self-satisfaction.

Post was sitting still, placidly smoking a cigarette.

Van der Valk sat down heavily in the chair opposite. "I am an honest man," he said. "I mustn't tell you I know yet exactly how to treat your case. My diagnosis isn't complete, I can see that. But of course, as always, recovery depends upon the patient in the end, hmm? Since you are evidently going to help me, I have confidence in your recovery. Well, we are both busy men, and I mustn't take up more of your expensive time. But next time we meet, I shall hope to find you on the right road, getting better."

Post said nothing at all. He just smoked his cigarette in a mannered careful way and looked at him amiably.

Outside on the pavement, Van der Valk shook his head at his own performance, so crude, so coarse, so uncivilized by comparison with Post's. I should be a fairground salesman, he thought; that's about my speed. Selling some quack cure-all in a pretty bottle to astounded villagers. Contains real gold, ladies and gentlemen, and only two-fifty for a half pint. Van der Valk the pitchman: live now and pay later. But there's no doubt that's the approach with a civilized type like the good Dr. van der Post. He felt mightily pleased with himself.

8

Next morning, back in the office, he was less inflated, less pleased with himself, but still feeling lucky. It was undoubtedly the weather, which he enjoyed, that made everything light and bright around him, that gave him energy and speed, that protected him from the landslide of gloomy depression that generally followed an early success in one of his affairs.

But no, really he couldn't help it, couldn't feel like a wooden police official, dependent on a mountain of administrative paper, surrounded by the querulous nagging of clowns like Chief Inspector Kan—not in this light that bathed Amsterdam in a dusty golden shimmer. The smell of green, of leaves, of shooting flowering bushes, was too strong, even conquering the sewer smell of the canal, and the inky-cardboard smell of the office. And Mr. Samson was on an island, and Scholten was in a tent, and that jugglebuggle of a Kan was lost somewhere in a perfect epidemic of auto thefts—cars that seemed mostly to belong to German tourists. Why was that? Was it simply that they contained a richer loot of money and passports, cameras and binoculars? Or was it some cunning notion perhaps masterminded by Cross-Eyed Janus? Van der Valk didn't know and didn't care, and if he were Kan, he thought happily, he'd go to Zandvoort and lie on the beach, and watch the German tourists playing with their expensive beach toys, and think with content of the unfortunate police of Cologne—even more swamped by the epidemic than they were here. Summer madness . . . August heat. Van der Valk, who had bought a paper bag full of plums on his way to work, wiped juice off his chin and felt happy. He had to go and wash; when he got back, he felt like making a nuisance of himself and telephoned Mr. Carl Merckel on his private line.

"Speaking." As though he didn't know that gray, guarded, neutral voice.

"This is Van der Valk. I'd like to see you. Before, during, or after lunch. Not knowing your appointments, I leave it open."

"You have something conclusive to say to me?"

"I've a slight case of sunstroke. Say the word."

"It does not sound as though I have much choice," vexed.

"No," blandly.

"I have no lunch appointment. At one o'clock precisely, be in the Chinese restaurant opposite the Concert Building."

Good heavens, thought Van der Valk, what extraordinary precautions to avoid being seen! He knew it well, an unpretentious place in need of painting, but the food was good; being much frequented by the musicians from across the road, it had to be.

"Sweet and sour everything—and lots of shrimp crackers," Van der Valk told the boy in the white jacket.

"Well?" said Merckel, still sounding vexed.

"I've taken up the matter you would probably have preferred me not to take up."

"How can you possibly know, or claim to know, what I prefer?"

"Why, I'll admit to you that the overwhelming impression I had when we met was of someone who wishes to avoid a responsibility and who makes a criminal indictment with every effort to minimize its possible truth or even likelihood," Van der Valk murmured.

"You do not know me well, I see. Inquire among

those of your associates who know something of the business world whether I am afraid of responsibility."

"If you did not have considerable moral courage, I agree, you would have kept silent altogether," Van der Valk said lightly. "There must be many things you would not be happy to have me know."

"I distinguished, I recall, between the private—and, I presume, discreet—knowledge of a police officer under oath and the public, uninformed insinuations of the press," Merckel said.

"That is precisely the position of my new acquaintance, Dr. van der Post. He does not mind my asking, guessing, even knowing all sorts of things as long as it is kept inside the walls of his consulting room. What might be said outside would be much less preferable, but he knows that I have no convincing evidence. He realized, however, that however disagreeable company I may be, I am a great deal preferable to the press."

"Are you telling me that my suppositions about this man are true but that you either cannot or do not propose to do anything about it?"

"Some of it is certainly true, I think. Even all of it, possibly. What you suggest might easily turn out to be the case. I might even say it happens every day," Van der Valk said tranquilly, with his mouth full of shrimp crackers.

Merckel laid down his soupspoon, wiped his mouth meticulously, and turned to look coldly at the policeman. "You give me an impression—I have no wish to sound offensive—of being decidedly lukewarm."

"I am lukewarm. I would warm up if I knew more things that I think have been kept from me. Have I, Mr. Merckel, all the information you can give me?

Suppose, for instance, I imagined the likely hypothesis that your wife had received blackmail threats also. And that she had gone to her Doctor, perhaps insisting that he remove the source of pressure and pain?"

Merckel looked, surprisingly, extremely shocked, as if this had never occurred to him. "She has a very strong sense of values," he said sharply. "She would have come to me, knowing that I would give her every support and that I would stand by her no matter what."

"No doubt. But in her loyalty to you she might think that none of this must reach you. That your position—your integrity, your honor; you have a very strong sense of honor—must not be smeared or even touched. Assume, by all means, that she would not think of any violent means of retaliating. She would then pay blackmail money, thinking it safer and easier to stand for the squeeze. How much could she pay without your noticing?"

"It's unheard of," muttered Merckel furiously.

"You see, it's not enough to insist on meeting me where no one would recognize you. It has not even occurred to you that I am—in different circles, I grant —as widely known a figure in this town as you are. Here, for example—in a place full of musicians—I might easily be recognized. I might even be seen by someone who would think it worth taking a little trouble to uncover your identity. You will have to get accustomed to numerous ideas, including that of my questioning your wife."

Merckel gave him a long look. Not furious or unhappy, but appraising, as though he were sizing up a man who had asked for the loan of money.

"Well, Mr. van der Valk," he said, at last. "I see that my notion that you would not show vigor was wide of the mark. You have evidently seen Dr. van der Post and apparently are not afraid of what he could do to your career. What conclusions you have really drawn from this visit are not my business. I now ask you whether you have thought what I can do to your career. As you remarked when I first met you, I am acquainted with a number of persons prominent in public life."

"Yet you still came to me. Perhaps you were sure that we would be careful not to probe too deep. If we were able to pin a crime—any crime—on the good Doctor, that would destroy his reputation and you would be content. But the idea of your wife being a likely suspect of a possible murder—and it was you, Mr. Merckel, who first mentioned the word—we would be too tactful to let that occur to us. Of course. You got the wrong man."

Merckel smiled contemptuously. "You have as mistaken an impression of me as most people have," he said dryly. "I am pleased that you do not allow yourself to be intimidated; if you did, you would be of singularly little use. If you wish to talk to my wife, do so by all means; I do not stand in your way. I ask you to respect my original wish for discretion and not to mention my name, even to her."

"Why shouldn't your name be mentioned?"

"That concerns me."

"I'll respect that." Van der Valk was careful to make no protest or further query.

There are a lot of things I don't understand in that quarter as well, he thought, having a little stroll; the trouble with Chinese food is that one invariably eats too much of it. I think I would almost have preferred it if Merckel had made more objection to my questioning his wife. He sounds pretty sure of her. Still . . .

He had to get an auto; Merckel lived out in Aerdenhout, on the far side of Haarlem. One of the creamy residential districts of Holland: elegant quiet streets lined with trees, down which purred elegant quiet autos lined with bank notes. The plebeian Volkswagen, in these streets, made a noise like the umbrella of classical tradition dropped on the floor of the British Museum. The streets wound aristocratically in and out of one another, noiseless but for the whir of lawn mowers: the villas all looked the same and all rather ugly, with cedars, plenty of grass, lush from the automatic sprinkler, a slight tendency to stained-glass and bulbous grandiosities, and a complete disregard of street numbers. He had the chance to admire a good deal of gaudy garden furniture strewn about among the cedars before he found the right house, and the usual Spanish maid to take his card, on the back of which he had scribbled, "I have just had lunch with your husband."

Mrs. Merckel was installed in one of those swinging garden sofas with fringes and a canopy, pretending to be reading *Ideal Homes,* with an eye cocked on his approach. He had expected her to try an icy-madam act, gaze fixed on his shoes. (They were quite expensive shoes, since any policeman is kind to his feet, but they needed mending and could have done with a lick of polish.) He was agreeably surprised when she jumped up lithely, offered her hand, and said "I am Mrs. Merckel; how do you do," in a voice that had a

56

pleasant warmth in it. "Do sit down. Have some orange juice?"

"Yes, please." She poured him a glassful, out of a Provençal earthenware jug that made a nice tinkling sound of ice cubes and had that primitive look he liked, as though it had been dug up in a field with bones of ancient Gauls.

"Cigarette? Oh, I love those ones of yours. May I have one?" It made a good impression, easy and unaffected and no kittenish gurgling.

She was a solid, well-constructed woman, not fat but all curves, with the very fine-textured pearly skin that goes so well with dark-chestnut hair. Small good teeth, quite rare in Holland, where the women have excellent teeth that look like well-polished rows of marble gravestones. A big wide comic mouth. She should have had large clear-brown eyes, but hers were small, with crinkles around them, and brilliant dark blue. He liked this face, and he liked her for not trying to hide behind the dark glasses, which she had taken off to look at him with a kind of honest curiosity.

"I must sound awfully inquisitive, but lunch with my husband sounds quite important, and I'm wondering where I come in?"

"That is quite easily told. My name is Van der Valk, I am an inspector of the recherche in the Amsterdam police, and trouble is my business, as Sam Spade used to say. Has anybody ever tried to blackmail you, Mrs. Merckel?" The well-known raid technique: the amiable little domestic pleasantry and the bomb in the same breath. Van der Valk, the smiler with the knife.

57

No, he could swear the reaction was genuine; she was too unguarded and too spontaneous. "I'm sorry . . . but talk about a bolt out of the blue. . . . Do you mean my husband thinks . . . ? Oh . . ." It had suddenly come to her to wonder why anyone should think she was being blackmailed, and she immediately looked stricken.

"Don't look so worried," Van der Valk said kindly. After the flash, the burn cream. "I think I know why someone might possibly have tried to blackmail you." She looked then with relief at him, wanting to be open but too cautious to put her feet in the water before she knew how cold it was likely to be.

"What has my husband told you?"

"Nothing. I told him. A little succession of things that had come to my notice, giving me the idea that an attempt of the sort might have been made." There was something rather dramatic about this talk, he thought. Blackmail, in this summery birdy garden, sitting on a padded swinging sofa on the lawn, innocently drinking orange juice with a pretty woman in primrose-yellow shorts and a white sharkskin shirt. It did not sound convincing at all. He didn't mind, because he didn't believe in it either. She was looking wary, but there was something transparent about this woman that was a most attractive quality.

"Did you ever hear of a man called Casimir Cabestan?"

"No. It sounds like a juggler in a cabaret."

"A painter—quite well known at one time."

"I'm afraid I don't know much about painting."

"Mrs. Merckel, I'm going to tell you quite honestly what I know about all this, and you can then tell me quite honestly whether it means anything to you, and if so, whether there are things I don't know or have maybe misunderstood." She laughed now. She had never heard of Cabestan—or Capstan, as Mr. Samson called him—and that made her think she was in the clear. It was evident that she thought he was driving at something else altogether, and was greatly relieved about it.

"I'm quite willing to try," she said amiably.

"This Cabestan—your husband knew him slightly, because some few years ago he did a portrait, it appears, for him—lived in a flat in Amsterdam, on top of a house owned by a Dr. Hubert van der Post. I say lived, because, you see, he is dead." The laughter went out of the eyes, and they glanced around nervously before she fixed them on the ground, pretending to be puzzled.

"I know Dr. Post of course; he has treated me. But I'm afraid I've never heard—"

"I'm going to put this quite bluntly, so please forgive me. The implication is that this man got the idea that you and the Doctor were too friendly, and was so certain he could establish this that he decided to try and make trouble."

"Have you told my husband this?"

"Yes. Your husband is interested in nothing but in supporting you, and if necessary protecting you. And so am I; it is what I am here for."

"Do you mean that Dr. van der Post complained to the police that this horrible man tried to—to get money from him—with this revolting tale?"

"No, Mrs. Merckel. The man is dead. He may have been a horrible man; we don't know yet. But he's dead, and when a man dies soon after an attempt to extort money, it may be a complete coincidence, but we do tend to believe that there may have been something in his story."

"You don't mean perhaps that you think I killed this man?"

"Hush, not so loud. No, I don't. It might be thought, not necessarily by me, that your husband did."

"But that's impossible. You simply don't know my husband. He's intensely scrupulous, very very upright—even if something—"

"Mrs. Merckel, the story is true, isn't it? You are, or have been, the Doctor's mistress?"

"Oh, my God. Yes."

"Listen, this is very important. Your husband—and I—wish to keep this whole tale from the public, the press, maybe even from a court, where you might be called as a witness, upon oath. He is as concerned for your good name as for his own. You must be quite straightforward with me; if you try to bottle up anything you know, you simply increase the risk of its coming out another way. Better me, your husband, a few lawyers than the press. Are you sure now that you know of no effort to blackmail you, or your husband, or the Doctor?"

"No. Honestly."

"Have you seen him in the last three weeks?"

"No."

"Phoned?"

"No. Wait. He did phone me, but only to ask whether I was all right. It's true—really—that I wasn't quite well, not ill, but not quite a hundred per cent, and he did make me better. He did call up maybe two or three weeks back; I couldn't say for sure. But he just asked whether I had any troubles."

"In those words—any troubles?"

"Well, I can't swear to the words. He might have said troubles, or bothers, or miseries—but meaning just was I all right."

"Or, possibly, meaning has anyone tried to blackmail you?"

"But—I suppose it could be twisted—but I knew nothing. How could I have guessed— God, what have I done?"

"Let me give you a piece of advice. Don't say anything at all to your husband unless he does, and I feel myself extremely sure that he won't. He will behave exactly as he always does. You do the same."

"But if my name gets in the paper?"

"It won't. Dr. Post has many patients. None of them would be at all happy if this business gets broadcast. The trouble is that someone was banking on exactly that fact. You get on well with your husband, don't you?"

"Very well indeed. This is the second marriage, you know, for both of us. Perhaps that's why some things appear strange. . . . " Her voice trailed off; she decided not to try to explain or justify.

"Neither of you has any children?"

"My husband hasn't. I have a daughter from my first marriage—she's sixteen now. She's studying art at the Royal College. But that isn't an obstacle between us, if that's what you're thinking. Carl is devoted to Suzanne, quite openly. Perhaps the more since he has none of his own. In fact, I'll tell you quite frankly, Mr. van der Valk, because I don't want any misunderstandings, if my husband's attitude seems odd to you it doesn't to me. He's fond of me, certainly, but if he appears—how shall I put it?—indulgent toward any failings of mine, it will be more for Suzanne's sake than for mine, or even for his, touchy though he is about his good name."

"Thank you, Mrs. Merckel. If I do have to come back again, I'll try and be very discreet about it. Remember what I said—be the same."

Attractive woman, he thought as he drove off. I don't know that I feel altogether quite so indignant about Dr. van der Post.

9

Before going home, he phoned an acquaintance, a man who owned a picture shop, a dealer and restorer in a small and specialized but skillful way, who always amused him. Charles was a lucky person, effervescent, with an enormous sense of the ridiculous and limitless ability to enjoy himself.

"Hello, Charles. No, don't tell me how you are; it takes too long. Are you well up on modern artists? Come, come, you move in the circle—you go to the parties, you can speak the absurd language."

"What circle?" Charles asked crossly. "There are dozens; they don't necessarily intersect." Charles' voice always came over the telephone in a high scream. "And there aren't any modern artists. There used to be a few but they've all run away to Paris like wise men. That was forty years ago anyway. Now all the modern ones are terribly old-fashioned and can only paint with torn-up dirty newspaper or bits of old bicycles. Deathly boring and totally unsalable. There is, of course, pop art. You want a quick course in pop art?"

"No. I want a quick course in Casimir Cabestan."

"That gin-sodden old fraud? There you are—went to Paris forty years ago, was stupid enough to come back, because he didn't get the admiration there he felt he deserved. Never been any good since, except for very young girls."

"What's this about girls?"

"Nobody knows. Cas looks every inch the revolting old wreck he is, but he possesses a sort of eerie appeal for tiny little girls of fourteen, whose blood he drinks. He generally has two or three in tow."

"Had, you mean. He's been dead nearly a month."

"You don't tell me. Well, all I can say is it really was high time. That just shows you—I have little or no contact with these circles, as you call them."

"Yes, but since you know about the tiny girls, you plainly saw him from time to time. You will know the stamping ground—perhaps where these famous tiny girls were collected, or paraded, or whatever."

"Oh, that. Yes, a sort of squalid dive they call the New Arts Club. Was probably new when Berthe Morisot was a tiny little girl. Now I've got it; you want to be taken? When? Tonight, if you like."

"It really is deplorable, this place," Charles was saying a few hours later; he was looking very fetching in a dark olive-green suit and an enormous yellow carnation. "It belongs perfectly to Casimir's era; one expects to see people like Ezra Pound all shaggy and youthful. Casimir fancied himself as a sort of painters' Scott Fitzgerald. I suppose we have to say 'Poor

Old' now instead of 'Dirty Old.' But the poor dears have nowhere to go. They still gather here and talk all excited about Trends. I haven't been here in a year. Now, who are you today, if I may ask?"

"I'd better be Mr. Petersen, come from Denmark, awfully keen about art. Do these types speak French?"

"Artists' French, fearfully twee. Here we are."

They had reached a very dingy entrance in a dingy street full of wholesalers, squashed in between the Damrak and the old quarter. The New Arts Club occupied a basement under a building filled to bursting point with, as far as Van der Valk could tell, old rags and papers done up in bundles.

"They're always praying there'd be a fire upstairs and then they could run away to Tahiti with the insurance money," said Charles. "They belong, you see, to the time when people really did run away to Tahiti. That's old Ben over there."

The light was excessively dim. Van der Valk distinguished a few eccentric haircuts, but was quite unable to say whether the persons under them were male or female. There was a candle stuck on the tiny bar in the grave of thousands of other candles, forming a dusty and discolored volcano of wax, and behind it loomed a disheveled man who looked about sixty, with a monastic hairdo, a goatee, a blue sailor's jumper, and mermaids tattooed on the backs of his hands. His face was quite weather-beaten, but in a pasty way, like one of the Pirates of Penzance who has forgotten to put his make-up on.

"Hello, Ben, how are you, old chap? This is a friend from Denmark, so let's all speak French, shall we?"

"Grand, my dears, grand. And how about a wee

droppie?" The voice of this square-rigger crimp was that of the eternal hanger-on, piping, precious. The tattooed hand sketched a coy arabesque in the air and a gin bottle appeared.

"Mr. Petersen was chatting about the old days and happened to mention Casimir, whom he knew before the war in Paris. We thought we'd find him here."

"Oh, haven't you heard? Poor, poor old Cas. Daid. Yais sir, daid." The voice had dropped into a sort of pretend-American, as though it thought it had strayed back somehow into Sylvia's Bookshop. "So tragic. Just a few weeks ago. Ah, Charlie, my dear, the old faces drop out one by one."

"Ben, I am not an old face, so don't include me. But what about the young faces? Surely there were some sweet young faces gathered around at the end?"

"No, no, he was all alone in the flat—heart attack. Young Harry Simons found him after nobody'd seen him for a day or two. As for the gorgeous lovelies, the last one I saw was a perfect pet. Cas called her his Sweet Sue. He brought her a couple of times to show her off, but she didn't really belong, you know. Amateur girl, Charlie, some rich pig's spriglet out slumming. Young Harry might know, of course, but we haven't seen him lately either. Got above the friends who gave him his start." Not a bad witness, thought Van der Valk professionally. They notice and record everything. You just have to know what percentage of that harmless tattling malice you have to discount.

"Well, well," Charles was saying. "That's all rather sad, isn't it, Mr. Petersen? Pity, pity, poor old Cas.

We'll have to be running along. So long, Ben, old boy. Give my love to Art."

"Any good?" asked Charles back in his white Renault coupé, which amused Van der Valk as much as the carnation did.

"I'd like to hear more about this Harry, and Sweet Sue. I want to find someone who knew the old drunk well in the last months."

"Yes, I see. Or, rather, I don't see but I don't intend to ask. Well, I can find Harry for you. Sue I know nothing of. I warn you, Harry Simons is a nasty little beast who thinks of nothing but money, and what I don't understand is his having any interest in old Cas, most of whose work changes hands for the price of the canvas."

"Tell me briefly and simply who Harry is," Van der Valk said.

"Harry is the son of old Simons, who was a good picture man and knew his stuff, and was respected by all. Had a gallery in Paris and one here. Got caught resisting and was turned into soap. Harry was a boy then, safe in America. Turned up a few years ago with a very bright line of patter—knew it all. The going in Paris was too rough but he flourishes here. He's quite a patron of these pop-art laddies and he knows that crowd in the cellar, but as Ben did not fail to point out, Harry cultivates old dames in mink coats and thinks himself a cut above the garret starvers. Cas, who is sudden death to a dealer and has been ever since the war, wouldn't be any use to our bright Harry. Get it?"

"I get it. Since you know him, can you work me in?"

"Sure. He's no friend of mine—runs around with

the pseudo-intellectuals. But I can phone him. Shall we see if he's in?"

"Yes."

"Luck," said Charles, coming back from a phone box. "In, and expecting you. I'll drop you if you like. You are keen on modern art. He's hooked, because he can't understand why I should pass such a bird on to him, knowing as he does that I hate his guts."

The flat was near the park, only two streets away from Dr. van der Post's brass plate. But this street was a lot less attractive; trees had been cut and speculative builders with more of other people's money than taste of their own had remodeled the houses into uninspired modernism. Van der Valk gazed at Harry's address, a large block of service flats without character or interest, trying to remember the limerick about the man who had phoned Miës van der Rohe.

Van der Valk went up in the elevator after he had found the apartment number among rows of mailboxes. The landing had a pale-violet carpet and orange-yellow walls; the elevator had had violet walls and an orange carpet; Van der Valk pressed a buzzer. A man of about thirty opened the door. He was dark and good-looking, with a supple fine-boned body. He didn't look particularly Jewish; he looked like a South American polo player. He was wearing jodhpurs with soft beautiful cowboy boots under them and an angora sweater, all in different shades of milky coffee. A blue silk shirt completed the color scheme of a Siamese cat. Van der Valk looked to see whether he had little silver bells around his neck but was disappointed.

"Come in, come in," he said hospitably. "Whiskey?"

"That would be very nice."

There were more luscious color schemes inside; the living room was dark dull crimson and old gold, with a white coffee table and white curtains. It was large and there was not much furniture, but plenty of art. Van der Valk sank languorously into a long long low low divan, clutched a glass of Stand Fast with a feeling that the name was inappropriate, and concluded that Mr. Simons mixed business with pleasure.

"Have a look about you," said Simons casually. "All this comes in and out very rapidly, of course, but while it's here, it's all for sale. Or have you some special name in mind?"

"Yes, I have, to tell the truth. Cabestan. I was wondering whether any of his early work was for sale."

Fine dark eyebrows arched at him. "I knew him slightly but I don't deal in his work. I understood from Mr. van Deijssel . . ."

"He didn't really know what the object of my interest was. I think that Casimir's been a little over-neglected."

Simons considered this with slow nods. "That could be. It might even be an idea. One might be able to revive some of his stuff, especially the early work, as you say. You could buy now and get a rock-bottom price. Why shouldn't we get together on this? I take it your aim is to encourage a market? I should be able to get some for you, I think. Starting perhaps with a particular line— What is your special interest—portraits, perhaps?"

"Girls," Van der Valk said.

"You mean nudes?"

"I haven't said that I was interested in buying pictures at all, Mr. Simons. I don't want to carry on this conversation under false pretenses. I am an inspector of police of the city of Amsterdam, and there are some queries I am making about this death. My special interest in Cabestan is girls, but not on canvas. Live girls. They can be nude or not, just as you prefer," pleasantly.

Harry took his time about sitting down and pouring out a whiskey; the decanter, thought Van der Valk, a squat Swedish thing, was a bad lumpy shape. He leaned back, glanced around, saw a piece of art that struck him as more obnoxious than most, and put his tongue out at it.

"I don't see how I can help you," said Harry warily. It didn't have to mean anything that he was wary; he was the type that always is, and suspects a trap most when there isn't one. This type is so dishonest that it is completely flummoxed by someone being honest. "I remember telling you that I knew him, but I saw very little of him and have no knowledge about his life."

"Before his death," Van der Valk said quietly, "Cabestan was seen around quite a good deal with a girl. A young and pretty girl—the kind I have heard he habitually had dangling."

"That's true," with a big open smile. "Old Casimir certainly did have a way of finding girls."

"You know this girl?" Van der Valk asked.

"My dear man, I hardly knew him, let alone his girls. I have a vague notion she is an art student of sorts. I have seen her, I think."

"It was you who found Cabestan dead, I believe?"

"Yes, it was," fluently. "I'd been after him some

time. I heard he had a whole bundle of drawings, early work by quite a few people he knew in Paris, and I was thinking of offering him a price for them. I couldn't make out why he didn't answer his bell, and I suggested at the house downstairs that he might be ill, and a sort of secretary person called the police. It was they, incidentally, who found him, not me. I was simply there."

"What is the girl's name?"

"Good heavens, I don't know. Or I can't recall. I was introduced to her at a party, I remember—Jill, Jennifer, something like that. I talked with her a minute or two—you know how parties are. I have a memory of a pretty enough girl, that's all."

"I see," Van der Valk said, grinning inwardly. "I'd like to find this girl, you see. I'd like you to throw your mind back carefully and remember who introduced you to her."

The silky eyebrows knitted handsomely. "There were several people there I know more or less well. I really can't tell for certain. It might have been Mrs. van der Post."

It was Van der Valk's turn to model eyebrow-knitting. "Really? Mrs. van der Post?"

"Yes, I dare say you know her. She's a good customer of mine."

"Isn't she the wife of some doctor?"

"I believe she is. I've never met him—don't know him at all."

"And was Cabestan at this party?" Van der Valk asked politely.

"I don't recall that he was. No—no, that's unlikely. I might be quite mistaken about Mrs. van der Post,

Cas being in my mind, you see, and the fact is that he lives in her house, up above. I might have imagined a connection that doesn't exist. I just remember chatting with her at that party."

"Who gave the party?"

Simons didn't quite like answering. "A television producer I know a bit—Arthur de Vries—out in Blaricum. But that's all three or four months ago. I'm afraid I really can't help you any more."

"That's all right," said Van der Valk generously. He really was content. This artistic cowboy wouldn't have told too many lies, because too much of his tale could be checked, and for all he knew Van der Valk had already checked.

"Just one final remark, Mr. Simons. It might be an excellent notion to try and create a market for nudes by Casimir, but don't get any idea of calling the press to get yourself a bit of publicity. It has a way of rebounding. And if any of the press get to hear that the police were interested in Casimir, I'd know who told them. Understand? And if I told that, there might be a whole lot of people not at all grateful to you. People who might be capable of doing your business a great deal of harm. All right? Just remember, keep your mouth shut." Harry Simons' bright black eyes had an odd expression that might have been knowing and might have been puzzled but was definitely quite intelligent in a faintly repulsive way. Van der Valk didn't think he would try to promote himself any press publicity. As for being cagey, these people couldn't breathe unless they were being cagey about something, but what on earth was there to be cagey about where Casimir's girl friends were concerned, and why should

Mr. Simons feel hot and bothered about "a pretty enough girl, that's all"? "A rich man's spriglet out slumming," Ben had said. It all sounded harmless enough, nothing to get evasive about.

Van der Valk walked the mile or so back to his home. It was a perfect summer night; everywhere on the streets there were crowds of gay, laughing, slightly drunken tourists. He felt curious, and somewhat inclined to pester Mr. Simons.

At home he undid his shoes, wiggled his toes, kissed his wife, and reached for the telephone book. Blaricum, hmm, out Hilversum way. He dialed.

"Might I speak to Mr. de Vries?"

"I'm afraid he's at the studio. If it's on business, you could try there."

"No no—personal."

"Well, can I take the message? This is Mrs. de Vries. Who is calling, please?"

"Oh, I'm a friend of Harry Simons'. I just came from his house. We were talking, as it chanced, about your husband."

"Oh, really? I was talking to Harry just a while back but he said he'd ring the studio."

"Ah, yes, must be the same thing we were discussing."

"Shall I give you the number, Mr.— I didn't catch your name."

"Don't trouble yourself, Mrs. de Vries; it'll do in the morning. Thank you so much again." He rang off and beamed at his wife, who had raised eyebrows.

"What were you putting on that affected voice for?" she asked.

"Ha. I've been moving amongst the intellectuals—

72

catching up with some modern art and picking up their little ways, don't you know?"

"It sounds awful when you do it. I don't mind Charles."

"Exactly. Dear Charles. He put me on to this. Let's ring him up. . . . Charles? I've had a nice chat with Harry. Don't worry, I said you knew nothing about it. But this girl of Casimir's—you know, this Susie— there's something funny there. Harry knows her, which wouldn't be noteworthy or even interesting. But he pretends he doesn't know her, and that is most interesting. He even rings up a fellow who knows something about it to enjoin him to be discreet. Any ideas about that?"

"I should just say he was being tricky out of force of habit. And people always lie to policemen."

"Yes indeedy. Especially when anybody has been killed. You see no significance?"

"What's a girl called Susie more or less? Old Cas always had a couple in tow—the usual vacuous teen-agers."

"Then why make such an elaborate pretense of knowing nothing about them?" Van der Valk asked.

"Oh, go to bed and stop fussing."

He put the receiver back, pleased with himself. "This is my night for being direct and blunt," he told Arlette. "Find me 'Simons, H.' in the book, will you?"

"Sounds like your night for collecting a phone bill. Why not do this in the office? Then you wouldn't have to pay for the calls."

"I just feel extravagant. Is there any milk? I'd like some cocoa very much if you could manage it. . . . Hello, Mr. Simons. This is Inspector van der Valk.

What? Well, no, the night's still young. How was Arthur? Hard at work boring the public? Now, I would like you to tell me the girl's name, please, and at once. Yes, that is all. My dear fellow, say just once more that you don't know and you'll find an invitation to headquarters on your desk tomorrow, which will bore you even more than it will me. No no, pal, I need no explanations. I need them not, I wish them not, I desire them not. It's Wilde? Thank you. Sleep tight. . . . Haven't we any whiskey?"

"Certainly not," said Arlette.

"Pity. I would have enjoyed whiskey. One more tiny call. Let's see, I've got the number written somewhere . . . hidden amidst all this evidence. . . . Hello? Mrs. Merckel? Inspector van der Valk. I'm very sorry to bother you. Entirely my fault. A tiny point of no importance that I should have asked you this afternoon, and stupidly forgot. Your name from your first marriage. Wilde? Thank you very much, and my apologies again for disturbing you."

10

Arthur de Vries was one television producer without a beard. He had rimless glasses, and a bright happy-to-know-you smile, and pale shiny skin. There were little cushions of smooth plumpness distributed all around his face, as though the bony bits needed something comfortable to sit on. A good deal of very white shirt covered a stocky body; he had, too, elaborately plaited and decorated moccasin shoes, and he liked to talk a kind of weird Hilversum-Manhattan

English, as though wanting to remind everyone that he had once made a trip to New York.

When Van der Valk arrived at the studio in Bussum, Arthur was very matey. "Come into the sanctuary and let's see if we can rustle up a cup of coffee." At home, no doubt, he would have martinis in a pitcher for the guests. He had been primed to be vague about anyone called Simons, so Van der Valk didn't mention anybody called Simons.

"Yes, I do recall a party. It was for my wife's birthday, but you know how these parties are."

"No, I don't. I'm not a great partygoer. That's what I've come for—so that you could tell me," Van der Valk said.

"Well, you know, these parties tend to fill up with people one may owe a bit of hospitality to—or people you regard as fairly interesting company but not much more. There might be thirty people you know well enough to say 'Hello, Joe, how's it going?' to, but only three you really know anything much about."

Van der Valk acknowledged all this worried apologia with the faint polite smile. "In which category would you put Mrs. van der Post?"

Arthur, who had been expecting a different name, beamed and became even more voluble. "Now, that illustrates perfectly what I mean, because I know her, yes, but just the way everybody knows her. Everybody invites her because she's one of the good mixers. Intelligent, bright, good-looking, poised—delightful woman. Knows everybody herself, no worry about having to run around bringing her into things. And knows all the stuff we're likely to be talking about. You know—she's really with it." It was delivered with whole-hearted approval; praise could have flown no higher.

Van der Valk decided to take lessons from this prodigious female. Be easy, engaging, disarming. If possible, be with it.

"Suppose, now," he said engagingly, drinking coffee, "she was a character in a play and you wanted to give me a sketch of her. You are hoping, perhaps, that I will finance a production or whatever. You want to make her very real, very convincing. How would you present her? Appearance, manner, character."

Arthur beamed some more, tickled with the notion. "Sounds like a party game. Still, let's see. She's well dressed in a rather formal way—always gloves, you know, and just enough good jewelry, and just been to the hairdresser. Must be in her forties, but looks younger—say, about thirty-five. Quite slim, moves well, nice quiet voice. Blond hair, bright, looking a little metallic but not artificial. Blue eyes that protrude a scrap. Good teeth. Very elegant, very poised. And let's see. She's calm, cool, gives an impression of balance and judgment—controlled, what you'd call unemotional. Doesn't smoke, doesn't drink. I suppose that all sounds dry, rather lacking in impact, but that isn't so. I'm fond of Bea; she's a grand person. She can listen to one's problems—you feel you can confide in her."

Arthur waved his cigarette through the air in a confiding pattern—he was getting quite carried away by his party game—and continued zestfully, "She's got no zing. I mean she's good-looking, but you don't think of her as attractive first and foremost. After three highballs, you wouldn't get the feeling of cuddling up with Bea, but you'd listen to what she had to say. She's reliable. And she's a grand temperature taker. I mean, say we were discussing a play or something, you might ask her, 'How did you think that little scene in the auto went?' And she'd say 'Too quick' or 'Too slow,' and you'd see at once she was dead right. I say, Inspector, I am talking a lot, though, aren't I? Poor old Arthur, they say, you can't stop him once he puts the nickel in. How did I shape up? Did I score high or low on the old projection test?"

"Not bad at all," grinning. "No need to worry about topping out just yet awhile."

"Ah, ha ha, you know the language, I see. You sure you don't mind if I have to dash off now, because it'll pile up there without me?"

"You go on right ahead," said Van der Valk. "The play's the thing wherein we catch the conscience of the king."

"Splendid, splendid," said Arthur approvingly, feeling very clever at having avoided all reference to Harry Simons.

It was all too neat, too pat, Van der Valk thought on his way back to Amsterdam. Each character linked so smoothly to the other, and all too much in a careful little pattern that would delight the heart of imbeciles like Arthur. Seven characters in search of an author.

Doctor has mistress, mistress has daughter, daughter knows painter, painter knows—presumably—Doctor's wife, painter blackmails Doctor. Cog slipping somewhere in that wheel.

Painter knows gigolo, painter knows daughter of Doctor's mistress. Gigolo knows daughter. Does painter know of Doctor's mistress through daughter?

Does gigolo know? Gigolo knows Doctor's wife? Does gigolo know of painter's little schemes? Are they even gigolo's little schemes?

This is exactly like a slot machine. We could go on all day and never hit the jackpot. Try another.

Painter blackmails banker, banker's wife sleeps with Doctor, banker's daughter knows gigolo, gigolo knows Doctor's wife. No further.

Doctor has possibly knocked off painter. Alternatively, Doctor has guilty knowledge of someone else knocking off painter. Who? Could be any of them.

Doctor is undoubtedly scared. Not very scared. Perhaps not scared at all and scared is the wong word. If scared, then perhaps not scared enough? Perhaps has nothing to be scared about really, bar scandal. Not very afraid of scandal. Too many notables involved. Doctor's notable patients, wife's notable family, banker's notable damn-near-everything.

Does gigolo know or has gigolo guessed anything about the blackmail?

There's no doubt about one thing: this play's not observing any classical unities. So much the worse for Van der Valk.

The sunshine was making him sleepy, and he yawned hugely getting out of his auto at the police parking lot. He was about to be rudely awakened by Chief Inspector Kan in a great state. Damn it, some important personage's Buick, a thing as long as a bus, had been stolen right here, just outside the Headquarters Building, while the owner was inside making a very strongly worded complaint about jewelry being pinched out of his hotel room. He, Kan, would worry about the auto; he was sure he knew all about that.

He, Van der Valk, would please see about this jewelry right away, because this was a very important personage, and the Swiss Consul had already been on the line and the Swiss Embassy would be any second now.

Van der Valk sighed heavily and trudged off. His play would have to wait—weeks, quite possibly.

11

Mr. Samson was back, offensively brown, bringing, as it were, a flavor of fish scales and sea water into the smell of paper work. The old man—it was one of his most likable characteristics—detested paper work and had a strong dislike of all written reports.

"I've done too many of those things myself not to know all the wangles that can be worked into a written report," he would often say, "Give me a verbal report, please." Administrative peccadilloes did not worry him, but his cross-questioning had a way of un-uncovering carelessness or downright stupidity that could be cunningly masked by the adroit bureaucratic phrase that pleased all magistrates very much. Even Mr. Samson could not stem the tide, of course. Van der Valk had once worked out that in an ordinary week he had spent fifty-eight per cent of his time writing reports (a stop watch on his desk and a neatly tabulated column of figures on the back of a memorandum about misuse of official stationery).

"Well," Samson said to Van der Valk after some grunting about the jewelry and the Buick, though both had been recovered, "what's been happening about your Doctor?"

Van der Valk had to consider. Really, he had

not given it much thought these past few days. It had almost been a holiday occupation, something to do while business was slack. A crossword puzzle? No, not that. The crossword mentality, adopted by many policemen he knew, who prided themselves on being "objective," was a fatal temptation. No, a play. That was as bad. Maybe it was worse.

"I think, really, there isn't a lot we can do. The more I poked about, the more of a hornet's nest I uncovered. I got a certain distance bluffing people with talk, but I can't get any further."

Did Mr. Samson have a very faint grin somewhere under his nose? Van der Valk . . . the best talker in the regiment.

"I've talked to the Doctor twice. He's very tense about something; I don't know whether he's nervous of me or not. He might have knocked off this painter, sure, and he might be more bothered at my poking about in a story where all the characters are interconnected in a very funny way. The painter turns out to have known a girl who is the daughter by a first marriage of this banker's wife, who was the Doctor's mistress. And he met her, got to know her, in a circle where this Doctor's wife is also a well-known figure. There is also a sort of coolness between the wife and the Doctor. All a mess."

"You aren't making it very clear," Samson complained.

"I'm not very clear about it in my own mind."

"You aren't thinking that the Doctor's wife may have been blackmailed, too?" asked Samson.

"No, I'm not. But anything is possible. The joker in the pack seems to be a sort of playboy art dealer who

80

knew the painter and even found him dead. Has a tale to cover that—not provable, not disprovable. This playboy knows the Doctor's wife, who is a shining light in these artistic-intellectual circles, and also knew the painter's girl, the other woman's daughter. He tried to gloss over that fact. I didn't like him, but I've got nothing whatever on him, either."

"So you're stuck."

"Yes. I'd got that far when this Swiss lark began, and I didn't like it then and don't now. This art boy is a type that is not above turning a profit out of anything. The blackmail idea may have come from him. He is in a good position. He knows the painter, knows —we don't know how well—the Doctor's wife, knows—equally—the girl who is the daughter of the Doctor's mistress. Now, all of a sudden, we find this girl in the company of the painter, deceased. They may have been introduced by the art boy, but the wife was also present. She may have done it, or the idea may have come from her. We don't know what knowledge to impute to her. Assume she has none at all and it sounds odd. Wife present at introduction of mistress's daughter to man who is, coincidentally, blackmailing mistress's husband and possibly—we've no proof or even a hint—her own husband. Impute any knowledge of her husband's goings on to her and it smells even worse."

"You mean that, knowing or guessing, she arranges a situation out of malice?" Samson asked.

"She might not know about any blackmail. She might have known about the mistress and tried to attack her through the daughter. This painter had a reputation for collecting young girls. On the other hand, she knew this art-dealing smoothy, whom the painter had known previous to all this. She may have given some grounds for blackmail herself. The painter may have been blackmailing two separate married couples and been suppressed by one of the four of them, as well as this boy friend who—it just so happens—found his body, in the flat above the house occupied by the Doctor and his wife."

Mr. Samson was sniffing and twisting his nose discontentedly. "All sounds very staged. Very melodramatic. Very artificial."

"Exactly what I thought. As though it had all been rigged expressly to throw dust in our eyes. And we haven't a damn thing on any of these people. Not even the art boy. He told me a couple of harmless lies, and so what?"

"So your wish, conclusion, deduction—ha—would be to withdraw."

"We've had absolutely nothing but a sort of backstairs accusation from the banker. I could, I think, show him now that he might be well advised to drop it. His wife was badly frightened and so was the Doctor. There's grounds for nothing at all but one of those old-fashioned ways of getting back at the fellow that's been sleeping with your wife—alienation of affection, or criminal conversation, or whatever it's called. And the banker would never make a formal complaint. He's not opposed to press publicity—oh, no, not much."

"Baldly, then, you're advising against further action of any kind, since you don't know what you might start, and you don't know where it might not stop."

"Yes," Van der Valk said.

"You called this young fellow, this art dealer, who according to you is slightly objectionable in a harmless way, the joker in the pack. You don't like him. You even think him capable of blackmail himself." Mr. Samson was speaking very heavily and laboriously, with puffs of cigar smoke between each phrase. He reminded his subordinate of an old rusty French steam locomotive that is perfectly capable still, when the mood takes it, of hauling a night express at a hundred miles an hour the whole way from Paris to Bordeaux. One sees him groaning and complaining horribly, bunting an endless line of stubby freight cars across the points of suburban marshaling yards. Suddenly he accelerated with loud puffs. "I see this girl more as the joker myself. The daughter. How old is she?"

"Sixteen." Van der Valk was greatly surprised.

"Sixteen. Uh. What does she know or guess or imagine, what mayn't she say or do, what mightn't she let out? Have you talked to her?"

"No," Van der Valk said stupidly, still astonished.

"Well, why not? If there's anything at all in this, she's the key figure."

"I've only just found out her identity. By accident. Picking up a little background on the painter, I heard this girl mentioned. Then the art boy didn't want to give me her name. When I did hear it, I was struck, but I didn't see how I could approach a girl of that age."

"But you agree that it's possible she might have played a part in contriving this stagy set of circumstances. Suppose, for example, that she learned something about her mother, mightn't she then have approached the Doctor's wife?"

"Anything is possible. Even a damn queer conspiracy. It's a family affair. We know about family affairs—huh—and the way the more one finds out, the more one becomes involved in things nobody can understand."

"Yes," said Samson slowly. "Pity the policeman who arrests an old woman accused of killing her husband in a small village."

"We might not be far off that right now," said Van der Valk.

There was a long sullen silence. Just so does the engine in the marshaling yard collapse into lengthy immobility for no reason any outsider can see. Dead stillness. Outside the window, a whole crowd of Amsterdam sparrows chattered and gibbered in a tree. Sun poured down, warm and cheerful, giving again that holiday illusion.

"I want to talk to this girl myself." Another unexpected burst of activity from the old engine. "I'm not going to decide whether or not to let you go any further into this till I have seen her. I'll send a polite note. No question of any interrogatory summons or anything judicial. A polite impersonal form. Where's my idiot boy? Blom! Blom, get a form, the one that says please present yourself with a date and time. Not the one saying failure to comply is punishable. In my name, here to this room. Van der Valk, you give him the address, and I'll want you here when she comes, to take notes."

"Leave out Motive," said Van der Valk. "Leave out

Commissaris and leave out Criminal Branch. Just put Room 25."

Blom, the secretary, who was not a real secretary at all but a trainee inspector learning administrative routine, put the form in one of those brown envelopes marked "Service," with a transparent panel in the front. Van der Valk, who was watching, extended his hand, removed the envelope, and handed the contents back. Blom seemed puzzled.

"Look," Van der Valk explained patiently. "You get one of these envelopes in the mail and anybody who sees it knows what it is. Which is sometimes a good thing and sometimes bad and most times indifferent. This time it is a good idea to avoid publicity. Take a plain white envelope, address it by hand, and trot out for a stamp, there's a good boy."

12

The form was sufficiently minatory not to be disregarded. "You are politely requested," it ran, in officialese, "to present yourself at Police Headquarters, Amsterdam. Please observe strict punctuality to the time mentioned hereunder. This form should be handed to the concierge on arrival." The concierge had been tipped off.

Van der Valk, sitting at the secretary's table, was struck by Suzanne's clothes. There is a lot of difference between a sixteen-year-old wearing blue jeans and a rebellious look and the same sixteen-year-old in a summer frock with stockings on and white high-heeled sandals, and Suzanne was carefully composed. She looked quite calm, was alone, and had appeared

85

on the dot. The face was pretty, young, and round. She behaved simply, as though she had been called up to the headmaster's office. Van der Valk was curious to see how Mr. Samson, who had an old-fashioned earthiness in his way with the public, would handle this girl.

The old man was going through some mail, which he shuffled into a pile and pushed aside.

"Good morning," he said casually. "Sit down, then, Miss Wilde." He picked up a neglected cigar and drew on it a couple of times to get it going. There was a sputtering noise and a red-hot fragment flew off the cigar. The old man killed it with a thick finger, wiping the cinders carefully away with someone's envelope. Fifth of November, thought Van der Valk. Or, as the French put it, fires of artifice. . . .

"Let me explain why I asked you to come and see me," began Samson quietly. "You probably, in common with most of the public, think of the police as concerned with nothing but crime, and if the average person gets a summons to the bureau, he starts examining his conscience and wondering what he's been caught at. Eh?"

"Well, I did wonder. . . ."

"There you are, you see. Nobody ever thinks that our function is always first to protect the public. And, of course, a good deal of that is the prevention of what is loosely called crime. Beginning with the local district police who pick up somebody who's been driving while drunk and lock him up for the night. That sort of thing has nothing to do with us here. If, however, they come across an involved tale, they call me, because they haven't the time to spend on unwinding complicated stories. You might call this the department of involved stories that may or may not have anything to do with crime but do involve the protection of the public. Eh? I don't suppose you've ever had anything to do with police, and that's why I'm telling you all this. Eh?"

All this paternalism seemed to be having the desired effect; the girl sat quiet and relaxed.

"Very good. These complicated stories drag in all sorts of people, whom we have to pester because they may have heard or known something that helps us to understand. People quite uninvolved in anything disgraceful. Clear so far? Good. Now it happens that a man died recently, and there are some surrounding incidental circumstances we aren't altogether happy about. They may have a perfectly simple natural explanation, and that's why we're trying to meet all the people who knew him, even slightly, and listen to anything however trivial or irrelevant they may be able to tell us. This man was a painter called Cabestan."

Watching her face, which he could see in profile, Van der Valk could not see anything beyond an increase in attention, perhaps. It was nothing more than the face of a girl practically of student age who is accustomed to concentrating on spoken words. To her, Mr. Samson appeared no more intimidating or important than her professor of Formal Design.

"You are an art student as I understand, Miss Wilde?"

"Yes."

"You go to a special school, where you learn languages and history and all the usual things, but with less emphasis on math and physics, and so on, but special courses in the development of art or whatnot. Is that all correct?"

"Yes." Her voice was small and shy, but apart from that she gave a poised, even an assured impression. She looked older than sixteen. One would have said eighteen, nineteen. Of course, these girls wear much more sophisticated clothes than they used to. They have their hair done professionally, they study their make-up carefully, and they all have that carefully cultivated air of worldly wisdom. Not really surprising, since these schools are forcing-grounds of their development.

"Was it through this artistic atmosphere that you met Mr. Cabestan?"

"No— Well, I should say not exactly." Polite girl's voice.

"Can you tell me how it was?"

"We have an art-appreciation class, you see, and we often get sent or taken to exhibitions. At one of these we were in a group with Dr. Geyl, who's one of our professors, and he introduced us to a lady who was there who knew him, and she was talking to me, and because of something she said—I don't know how to explain—she took me to someone's house. . . ."

"Apropos?"

"Yes, that's it, apropos—Well, a house where there were some pictures and I met Mr. Cabestan there."

Never thought to see the old man being so patiently gradual, Van der Valk told himself. One learns something new each day.

"The lady is called?"

"Mrs. van der Post. She knows an awful lot of painters and dealers and—oh, everybody."

"The house belongs to her?"

"No, a sort of dealer. A Mr. Simons. Well"—in rather a hurry—"Mr. Cabestan was there, and he was making jokes about a picture they all thought was good and he said was no good. And he asked me, more or less as a joke, whether I thought it was good, but I wanted to be serious and I said no, to be honest, I couldn't see it, and he laughed like anything and told me I had good taste. Mr. Simons was rude and said he was about as far behind modern taste as Ary Scheffer—Mr. Cabestan, I mean. I rather liked him. And then Mr. Simons gave us a drink and said I had a lot to learn and I shouldn't listen too much to Dr. Geyl and—well—it just happened I got to know Mr. Cabestan. I can't really explain any more."

"You don't have to," said Samson composedly. "That's perfectly clear and reasonable. So you saw a bit of Mr. Cabestan from then on."

"Oh, yes, he took me to a few places, and to see his own work, and was always amusing and funny, though I thought, to be honest, he talked awful nonsense about most things."

"Um. And do you think he was just anxious to teach you about art?"

She laughed. Without affectation, perfectly naturally. "Of course not. Oh, he talked about art all day, but he wanted to make love to me, of course. He was always trying to get me to pose for him."

This directness in the rising generation disconcerted the old man a bit, and Van der Valk had to grin. "In the nude?" he said a bit awkwardly.

"What else? I didn't, naturally. But I liked him in an odd way. He was a poor old fellow—nobody took him very seriously, I could see, but he had nice sides, too. I thought he was even a pretty good painter once. He drank too much."

"And did you ever meet Mrs. Post again?"

"Yes, outside his house. I was there three or four times. He used to get amorous but I used to sort of shake him loose. Later I found she lived there—downstairs, I mean. It's a big house. She said hello very nicely and asked me to have coffee with her in town. And I met her once at a party."

"Did Mrs. Post know Casimir? I mean she obviously knew him, but was there a closer acquaintance?"

She laughed again clearly. "He couldn't stand her. He called her the art whore. That was just spitefulness, of course, because she despised his work."

"You liked her yourself, though?"

"Like? I don't know her well enough. She was always polite and nice to me, as I say," the girl said a little impatiently, as though she found the old man rather obtuse.

"She knew that you were friendly, or acquainted, with Cabestan, at least?"

"Oh, yes, of course. There wasn't any secret about it."

"So your parents knew it as well," Samson said smoothly. Not quite so obtuse. First tiny sign of hesitancy and confusion in the girl's manner. Van der Valk, quietly writing shorthand, could see her very well.

"Now . . . to be honest, no. I mean they're very reasonable about letting me go where I please and meet whom I choose, especially when it's anything to do with work, but—well, it's a question of tact, really. I mean if I'd mentioned Casimir at home, there might have been a discussion and questions and it might have led to a row, and I just prefer to avoid that."

"That's quite natural." It was decidedly the first time Van der Valk had ever known the old man to be silky.

"Would both your parents have been inclined to disapprove?"

"Perhaps," she said carefully. "My father's more strict but he has to be because he's very well known, you see. My mother wouldn't really have minded much but she'd back him up, if you understand."

"But you find it reasonable that she should back him up, eh?"

"A wife ought to back her husband up," she said immediately.

"Have you ever met Dr. Post?"

Again a hesitation and this time tension. Slight, and noticeable only because her answers had been coming so easily.

"Well—'met' isn't quite the word. He treated me a couple of months ago for anemia."

"I thought he was a neurologist."

"I don't know. My mother says he's a good doctor. He certainly cured me."

"Ah, your mother suggested it. I don't know why; I thought perhaps Mrs. Post had suggested your consulting her husband."

"No no," emphatically. "She knew nothing about it."

"She never introduced you to her husband?"

"I'd never seen him. I supposed he wasn't interested in pictures. That is to say, I'd never thought about it."

"Um. You know Mrs. Post and your mother knows Dr. Post, but your paths just hadn't crossed, uh?"

She looked a little puzzled. "I don't think my mother knows him all that well. She'd consulted him one time, she told me, and I suppose she found him good."

"Exactly. Now, this Mr. Simons—did you ever meet him again?"

She was going to balk; he could see it. Mr. Samson lit another of his terrible cigars. Van der Valk got a cigarette out one-handed, awkwardly.

"You are pretty inquisitive about all my doings, aren't you?"

"But that's our work, you see. Just like painting pictures, or building a wall, come to that," Samson said, poking with his burned match to get a better draft in the horrible thing.

"Can't you tell me what it's all about, then?"

"I may," said Mr. Samson briefly. "We'd got to Mr. Simons."

"I met him a couple more times. You know how it is—you get into a sort of group."

"You've been to his house again?"

"I don't know who can have told you that."

"Nobody told me. That's why I ask."

"A couple of times, yes," the girl admitted.

"When was it that you heard Cabestan was dead?"

"I hadn't heard anything of him in awhile and I supposed he'd just got tired of trying to make me. A couple of the boys told me he was dead. It was a shock because—it always is, isn't it? I mean hearing someone is dead. I mean one knows people die, of course, but you don't expect people you know ever to die. But I wasn't terribly surprised, because I knew he wasn't well. He drank much too much, and he used to go a funny color and breathe heavily after climbing all those stairs."

"You said a couple of the boys?"

"Yes, at school, but not the same class. They heard at the Arts Club, they said. Casimir used to go there. He took me once, but I didn't care for it—all that unwashed crowd of pseudos."

Mr. Samson, beginning to look more recognizable to Van der Valk now, made another of his swerves. "Did your mother know you had met Mrs. Post? You would have had no special reason to be tactful about meeting her, I take it?"

"Well, I suppose not, but I don't think I ever mentioned it. I suppose it just never came up," lamely.

"I see. . . . Did you know that Simons found Cabestan dead?"

"I haven't seen Mr. Simons in quite awhile." Her voice was very cold.

"But you knew the two were friends."

"I don't know anything of the sort. I don't think they were friends."

"Why do you say that?"

"I don't know. . . . Casimir never talked about him as a friend—not to me, anyhow."

"He talked about him, then?"

"Oh, well . . . because we'd met at his house . . . I really hardly know Mr. Simons."

"I get the impression—correct me if I'm wrong—that Mr. Simons is not a pleasant subject of thought to you."

"I don't care for him much."

"Had he ever made any advances toward you?"

"No." She blushed. She hadn't blushed at Cabestan's advances being mentioned.

"Cabestan and Simons hadn't perhaps had a disagreement—maybe about you?"

"Not that I know of."

"And you wouldn't know why Simons went to Cabestan's house, on the occasion he found him dead?"

"No. Are you suggesting someone killed Casimir?" Suddenly. Had it really only just struck her?

"Somebody would like us to believe that." His voice was very calm.

"And you think it might have been Harry Simons?" The intonation sounded as though the thought did not displease her. Samson did not answer; he knocked the ash off his cigar.

"You don't think I killed poor old Cas, for heaven's sake?"

"You'd prefer we thought it was Simons, no doubt," without irony. She wriggled, disconcerted. She was looking a lot more her age now.

"Mr. Cabestan," he said dryly, "had been blackmailing your father. Demanding money from him on the strength of a pretended secret that would cause your father great embarrassment if it were to become public. Any idea what that would be?"

She went flaming scarlet. "My father knows— No, Casimir. . . ."

"Yes, Miss Wilde? You must tell me. This is extremely important. What did your father know?"

"That I. . . ." Freeze. "No—Casimir *didn't* know," desperately; it was a wail.

"Yes, Miss Wilde?"

She burst into hysterical sobs. Samson made a face

at Van der Valk, who got up and came back with a glass of water. He put it on the desk; she sent it across the room with a furious slap. Neither policeman paid any notice. Blomboy, as Mr. Samson called him, could mop that up.

"That Cabestan had seduced you, Miss Wilde, I think you want to say."

"No! No! No!" Mounting inflection of passionate emphasis. Van der Valk suddenly opened his mouth wide, got a nasty look from his superior officer, and shut it again hurriedly.

"Van der Valk, make out an official form of interrogatory summons to Harry Simons."

The girl gave a great gulping sob, straightened up, and looked at him terrified.

"Harry Simons had seduced you, Miss Wilde." She made an effort and nodded. "That was what your father knew?"

"I would like some water."

"Van der Valk."

Sighing slightly, he had to go and get another glass. There wasn't one, but he found a teacup.

"I'm sorry if I sound inexorable," said Mr. Samson quite kindly. "I do not wish to bully or frighten you. This won't last much longer, but we must have these facts. Of course, nobody suspects you of anything criminal, not even knowledge of anything. But I must know the truth. Would you like some more water? Very well. Simons seduced you. Cabestan was jealous, I think."

"No. He didn't know. Not from me, anyhow."

"Good, he didn't know. You encouraged him a little—I see—to help make a break from Simons. No, all right, that doesn't matter for the moment. Ah. . . . Did Simons by any chance become a little jealous of Cabestan? Think maybe that you were too familiar with him? As I have heard, Cabestan had a bad reputation with young girls like yourself, and what you say about telling your parents rather confirms that you knew that—eh?"

She nodded hesitantly. He thought for awhile and then made up his mind.

"Very well, very well. I've no wish at all to seem rough with you, Miss Wilde, and I'm sorry you've had a hard time. It's over now. If you like, there's a washroom along the passage. Thank you very much for coming and for being extremely helpful. You're free of course to go, whenever you like. Show her, Van der Valk. . . . By the way, Miss Wilde?"

She turned, still dazed from tears.

"I don't think you'll want to say anything about this at home, will you? Did you mention that you were coming here to see me?"

She shook her head.

"So much the better, then. I'll say nothing about it, either, to your parents. Eh? That console you a little?"

"I won't say anything. You mean it, really? You won't tell my father I was here?"

"No, I won't. You have my word."

When Van der Valk got back, Mr. Samson was trying to read his shorthand. "Type this up. I want to read it."

Meekly, Van der Valk sat down at Blom's typewriter.

13

Mr. Samson read the transcript carefully; Van der Valk, with the carbon, did the same. There was silence broken only by the old man's characteristic trick of taking his glasses off, throwing them on the desk with a clatter, staring out of the window, heaving a sigh, and putting the glasses on again.

Van der Valk thought about Mrs. van der Post, whom he had never seen. That imbecile De Vries had undeniable talent. There was something vivid about his ridiculous "sketch" that could be seen more clearly after listening to the remarks of a teen-age girl, more vivid still because she had not only talent but the perceptive naïveté that opened windows on obscurity as nothing else could have done. He was full of admiration for Samson, who had known this without ever having met any of these people.

Was it purely coincidence that Mrs. Post had crystallized the interrelation between these people? If the girl had not met her at a gallery and through her Simons, she would never have met Cabestan, who had plainly detested the Post woman—"the art whore." Had Post himself had any idea of all this? He had treated the girl for anemia, but had he seen anything in her except the daughter of a woman he knew? His mistress, certainly, but was that important?

Had Casimir seen the girl in or leaving Post's house? Had that given him ideas or suspicions? The girl had been important to him; she gave him, plainly, a new lease on life. And perhaps his death.

Simons obviously counted for nothing. He might

have been used as a pawn by the Post woman. Poor fellow—what a blow to his self-esteem! It was possible that he had known or guessed something of Casimir's maneuvers. La-la-la-la—who would ever know who had maneuvered what and why? If Casimir was attached to the girl, would he really have decided to blackmail her father?

"You don't want this Simons picked up, do you?" Van der Valk asked.

"Of course not. That was a squeeze on the girl. One point in her tale rings false. She was seduced by Simons, who is plainly a sort of professional narcissist spending his life admiring his own magnificence. She learns to detest Simons, and in reaction Cabestan comes to appear to her a likable person. That is all consequent enough. Then we find her suddenly going to this Doctor, to be treated for anemia. That I don't find consequential. In the same house, though she rather disliked the wife, whom Cabestan, moreover, loathed, and whom she had a grudge against—the person who had mixed her up with Simons."

"The mother—" Van der Valk began.

"You don't send your daughter for treatment to the man who is or has been your lover," decisively.

"Everybody agrees that, whatever his morals, he's a good doctor."

"No no no. If the mother really sent her, there's something behind that. I think she went off on her own." Samson took his glasses off again. "The other thing that doesn't satisfy me is the whole attitude Merckel takes up. Look at the chain of events.

"Cabestan learns in some way, possibly through the daughter, who may know or guess—impossible to say whether she was acting when I asked her—that the mother is Post's mistress. He is attached to the girl, but something sours it and his resentment fastens on the whole tribe of Posts. He decides for reasons of his own to put the bite on Merckel. I wonder why.

"Now, Merckel has every reason to keep quiet about this, and does in fact keep quiet about it. Cabestan dies. Merckel then comes to us with an absurd tale about a scruple. He accuses Post of killing Cabestan, and he never tells us what grounds he has, since all he has to go on is Cabestan's tale that his wife is Post's mistress, a fact that by his own admission he cared little about, provided she was discreet. He must have had something more to go on. That something is certainly to do with the daughter. You heard her. Her father knows something about her. And you tell me that the wife's evidence was that Merckel is very attached to his stepdaughter, having no children of his own."

"But if he found out she had been seduced by Simons, how would that rouse him against Post—or Cabestan?"

The old man regarded Van der Valk with dislike. "I know nothing. I've never seen any of these people. I have nothing whatever but the girl's words to me, and I'm trying to find a logical explanation for them. Since you apparently haven't had the patience to think about these things, I have to do it for you. I see a fact.

"A month or so after the girl has an affair with Simons—call it that for a convenient formula—she goes to Post, of all people, to be treated, we are told, for anemia. I can't swallow that."

Van der Valk, who had swallowed it, was abashed.

"Suppose—suppose—she went there herself, possibly giving some excuse to the mother, and asked Post for an abortion. Thinking possibly that she can twist Post's arm, knowing a few things either from the mother or through Cabestan."

"Even if it were true, we'd never prove it. Couldn't use it against Post without a fearful stink," Van der Valk said.

"Yes yes, you don't need to tell me," irritably. "Nobody's proposing to use it or even mention it. But if it is true, it explains what does not at present ring true. Merckel, either from the girl or more likely from Cabestan, finds out something of this. He may even have thought Cabestan the putative father, and that he had sent the girl to Post. In which case they are both birds of a filthy feather, and when Cabestan suddenly dies, Merckel concludes that Post has removed an awkward and disagreeable accomplice. And that sticks in his throat. The fellow has attacked him, his wife, and now his daughter, and that goes too far. He comes to us with hints but tries to suppress any mention of the daughter."

Van der Valk, who had thought Merckel was holding something back and had wondered why the banker should be indifferent to his approaching the wife, was impressed by the old man's grasp of a situation that had baffled him. But was the old man really proposing to do anything about it?

"We can't use this girl as a witness against Post," Samson went on. "And we can't begin any legal action. But you've talked to this fellow a couple of times now. You might see whether there was anything that could be built up there. Don't try to intimidate Merckel. All these people are in a position to make life very difficult for us—bear that in mind, lad. Look at all this mess on the floor. Where's my Blomboy?"

14

Mr. Samson would say no more. Van der Valk knew. Either now or at any other time. It was up to Van der Valk now. If he reported—after a decent interval for mourning—that there was nothing to be done with any of these people, the old man would take the whole file, bury it in a hole eight feet deep, and never mention it again.

There was nothing he could do with Heer Merckel.

There was nothing he could do with Mrs. Post, either. He had nothing whatever against her, and the moment he tried to question her she would smell a rat. The woman from the powerful family of magistrates, the shining light of intellectual circles, "the art whore"!

As for Post, he had been right outside Van der Valk's book and powers from the word go. If Post lifted a finger, his job was gone. Post must know this. Why hadn't he complained? Better still, why hadn't he simply thrown Van der Valk out?

And yet—what was the streak of fatalism or obstinacy that made Van der Valk persist?—he didn't give up. Quite the contrary, he phoned for another appointment. Devil take it, how stupid he sounded. Would that secretary really not be suspicious this time?

"I'm afraid," he said cautiously over the telephone,

"my trouble still hasn't cleared up. I would like to see Dr. Post again, as soon as it can be managed."

"That's quite all right, Mr. van der Valk, I understand. Afternoons still suit you best? Let's see . . . you could come tomorrow. It's lucky that it's August, you see. Very many of our patients are on holiday, and don't want to think about disagreeable things like appointments," she said sunnily. Her voice was quite innocent; Post could have said nothing to her. No, certainly not.

"Many thanks," he said. "That'll do very well indeed."

15

"Me again," Van der Valk said, in a voice stupidly bright that he would have sworn was not only false but practically falsetto.

"Must be the heat," remarked Dr. Post calmly. "Nervous troubles are precipitated by a heat wave; it's a commonplace."

Indeed it was hot; it had gone on and on undiminished. Asphalt stuck to the soles of everybody's shoes, and fat Amsterdam housewives had given up wearing dresses altogether, and hung out of their windows in slips as shiny and violently colored as lollipops, languidly shaking out their dusters and showing a good deal of unaphrodisiac armpit. The sales of fizzy lemonade had reached such dizzying heights that the factories could not keep up with the demand, and the owners did not know whether to laugh happily at their monstrous profits or shut the phone off to stop the shower of complaints. And the Amsterdam police force was in trouble, too. The uniformed members were hoarse from protesting because some unusually lunatic city father had decided that with all the tourists around the police had to keep their jackets on. "Shirt sleeves," had run his peroration, "are not only unhygienic and undignified; they are a blot upon our good name in far countries."

In Dr. Post's consulting room, it was cool and delicious. One was deeply grateful for the solidity of old-fashioned houses, for the thick insect-haunted shade of the lindens outside that shed a kind of sticky deposit on the pavement, above which spiders clambered up and down their ropes with charming agility.

Dr. van der Post was certainly unaffected by heat. His suit was perfect, his shirt had an elegant cut, his untroubled eyes had their warm smiling sympathy.

"I like the heat, myself," said Van der Valk.

"So do I. It is rare. And precious if on that count only."

"Cabestan's flat must be pretty hot on a day like this."

"I dare say."

"I'd be interested to see that flat."

No answer. Post took a cigarette and lit it, weighing a slim lighter in his long well-shaped fingers as though meditating the pros and cons of something.

"What plans do you have for the place? Going to find another artist as tenant?"

Suddenly the Doctor got up, surprising Van der Valk, who was by now used to immobility and indifference. "Come and see for yourself. Satisfy your curiosity. I'd prefer to have no secrets from you rather than to find a legion of spies observing my movements,

103

gossiping with my chauffeur. I wish to put a stop to this curiosity of yours."

He walked out into the hall, a tall man moving quietly.

Van der Valk followed him to the street, where Post took a key ring from his pocket and stopped to look at the lindens. "Considerable insect population—I'm quite surprised to see no policemen up there." He opened the door at the corner and motioned Van der Valk to go first. There was threadbare stair carpet, steep steps within narrow walls, flight after flight. A twenty-five-watt bulb at each narrow landing. One story, two stories, three, then a painted deal door. The landing was lit by a skylight, but the big studio had mansard windows as well, and enough daylight came in for any painter. Curtains were now drawn against the sunlight—stained and faded beige cretonne that had once been yellow. It was hot, stuffy, and somewhat dusty, but not as bad as Van der Valk had expected. A spider sat motionless in the ceiling corner and a big daddy longlegs had taken a post on the curtain rail, but the place did not seem totally deserted or neglected.

Van der Valk realized that someone had swept, even dusted, done something to make it habitable. And had spent time there. Whose was the glass and the bottle of mineral water? Whose was that elegant silk dressing gown? Not Casimir's.

"Ah, I see you've taken up camping."

"I did not, you may imagine, wish you pawing about among my possessions without my being there to keep an eye on the performance," the Doctor said coolly.

"Rather pleasant."

"I have a certain taste for solitude."

"Yes, I've noticed. Even doing your own cleaning. No women allowed up here." He was looking at the books with interest. What was this?

Police work is not a great encouragement to intellectual interests. And Van der Valk's education had been nothing spectacular. But he was in no sense the sheep that looks up and is not fed. More like the goat that, having devoured all the rosebushes in sight, gets busy with the neighbors' vines.

Van der Valk's father had been a carpenter whose hobby was cabinet making; by the time he died, he had even taught himself marquetry. He had gone on a three-day trip to Paris, had stood openmouthed in the Louvre, and for the rest of his life had been full of Oeben and Riesener, Leleux, Weisweiler, and Molitor, mispronounced but thoroughly understood.

His mother had, in her own words, "bookwormed herself through the whole damn public library." It was not really surprising that he had become the kind of person who could not pass a book without picking it up.

One of these books caught his attention. The author's name was Van der Post! When he picked it up, it seemed familiar. Yes, it was about Africa; he remembered it—a vivid book, by an expert, just the kind of man he liked. There was a phrase in it that had lodged in his memory, too. Something about the individual—one must learn to work out one's individual problems, and see every other man as an individual, and only when that had been done would it be time to do collective thinking, about people in groups, people as groups.

Van der Valk picked up another book, and was immediately curious about it. What was this? Myth? Elves and dwarfs and goblins—did Dr. Post have fairy stories by his bed, then? Yet it seemed to be an adult book. He sat on the divan absorbed for some time, looked up suddenly, and saw Post at the other side of the room. He had hung a picture on the wall, and was now standing back judging the effect.

This Doctor lived among objects of perfect taste, in luxury, well away from the smell of cheap shops and ugly objects, away from sweaty people with shapeless shoes crowded around sale counters. What did he like about this half-sordid, shabby room, with its smell of old sun-heated paint and cheap linoleum and paraffin? A heap of rubbish that someone had looked at and decided was not worth the effort of carting away. What was so attractive about it to this man, who was even sleeping up here on a cheap divan carefully made up. A whimsical fantasy? Was that the way a man acted who had killed the last inhabitant of the bedraggled flat?

Van der Valk didn't know. He would have to think about it. And Post was just standing there looking amused.

Van der Valk beat a retreat, hoping he didn't appear too disconcerted.

16

In the street, however, his detachment switched on, like the photoelectric cell that lights the street lamps at dusk. Certainly, he thought, I must look exceedingly ridiculous. Both there in Post's house and right here in the street. Like the classic caricature of a German tourist stopping to gaze at buildings of great antiquity and hideous ugliness with cloud-wrapped piety, he had just caught himself raptly reading a torn poster for an exhibition that had been held a month ago.

When nearly home, he went into his local book-shop, where several people were standing transfixed, studying the latest pornographic fiction, oblivious to their surroundings. The owner, who knew Van der Valk well, was leaning on his counter, looking maliciously at these sad people.

"Two ball-points, one red, one green. . . . Come on," Van der Valk said, "there are cheaper ones than that. . . . Do you know a book called *The Lord of the Rings*?"

"Sure. I have it in stock, if you want it."

"You have? Let's see. . . . This a best-seller or something?"

"No no. I buy one at a time and it sells every month—has for years. Specialized appeal. I've read it —a totally new world, landscapes, languages, history, all complete. It has all the things people like—war, poetry, kings, castles—and it leaves out everything they have to live with. No money, no sex, no commerce, no industry. Remarkable and very imaginative. It's not like anything else; it's a phenomenon."

Van der Valk stood for three-quarters of an hour, quite as transfixed as the students of pornography. When the bookseller told him so, he was so cross he bought the book.

What was more, he sat up half the night with it.

107

Strange thing for a Dutch policeman. It was English, of course; a Frenchman would not write like that. But a German would like it, too—rustic humor and pastoral verse, many songs and rhymes, mountains full of wizards and romantic horrors, a hero in armor and a pale princess. Just the book for Ludwig of Bavaria, but one would hardly have thought it was for a specialist in women and neurology.

The author had a strange name, not very English-sounding. Tolkien. That could almost be a Dutch name. Which was remarkable.

The national character, he thought vaguely, is a thing about which a lot of nonsense is spoken and believed. They are very proud of what they call "sobriety"—spoken of daily as the national virtue. "Looking at both sides of the penny," "down to earth," "you can't fool me." Determined to see what is, and to detect, and to abolish what only might be. It leads to a hateful caution, a loathing of imagination, a fear of fantasy. If hypocrisy is the English vice, and vanity the French vice, and obedience the German vice, then surely sobriety is the Dutch vice.

It was four in the morning. His wife had gone to bed indignant with him. It couldn't be helped.

"Tolk" in Dutch means an interpreter. "Ien" is a diminutive. Had the man or his ancestors gone to England? That other Van der Post, the African one—his grandfather had run away, too, from Holland.

Why did the Doctor go and live in the top-floor studio where poor old Cabestan, an unsuccessful painter, had died? Was this Doctor something of an unsuccessful poet? Being a successful doctor might be a strain on the man? Why had he married a woman from a family of magistrates, with artistic tastes? That first-pressing of the grapes of a bourgeois nation, where all the aristocracy and all the tramps had been most carefully, conscientiously throttled, years and years ago. Did the Doctor deliberately choose and seduce women from the same background?

With his head full of dwarfs and goblins, Van der Valk took a long while getting to sleep.

A police department is a rigid hierarchy, like any other civil-service branch. Van der Valk, an inspector, was a captain. Under him came a crew of noncommissioned officers and simple soldiers given a special training to distinguish them from the common run of police, who have never been better described than they were by Fouché a hundred and fifty years ago. Whores, thieves, and street lamps.

Van der Valk disliked the rigidity of the hierarchy. To take an example, the "filature," or throwing of a net of policemen around any individual whose habits and movements one may wish to study, is entrusted automatically to flatfeet, whereas, Van der Valk thought, it is a very difficult and delicate undertaking. However, this time, he could do it himself—he had to do it himself—in his own time, at that.

Not only was Dr. van der Post not official business, but also he was a man on the lookout for insects in the linden trees.

17

He had been wondering for some time where he had seen the man before. The dandified narrow suits, the long elegant hands, the delicate gesture pushing the handkerchief up the sleeve to avoid any wrinkle or bulge in the jacket. He was familiar from somewhere with that long neat head, the stiff hair cut short with what would be a fringe were it not suddenly combed sidewise to present a level untroubled forehead. The eyes perceptive and melancholy, the wide mouth with its perpetual mocking smile, the large well-modeled ears.

Once a week, Van der Valk went to a sort of athletic club that featured the less popular, almost snobbish sports—fencing, badminton, squash. Some of the judo boys trained there, and a few of the physical-fitness fiends who went in for the formal ballet-like rituals of gymnastics. It was a nice place, with a tiny pool such as one finds in a Turkish bath, and one heard the sporting gossip of Europe there. The rates were high, but Van der Valk did not mind; one got to know all sorts of amusing people. He was no earthly good at games, but was active and resilient enough to play most of them with enjoyment, and it was nice after sitting cramped over some thirty-page pomposity of a report all afternoon to box a bit and then go headlong into the little pool and come out with a villainous thrash that a friend, a backstroke champion, called the Harbor Police Special.

Up till now, Van der Valk had hardly noticed the Doctor, and the Doctor had certainly never noticed him, because Post belonged to the club's exclusive, fastidious clique, which had a special room with proper lockers. A few other specialist doctors and lawyers used the special room, too, and a brace of high municipal executives, a Consul, and a concert singer. They did not dream of playing with riffraff like businessmen or television stars. Squash was their game. Dr. Post was rather good, with venomous shots coming back at totally unexpected angles, and that spectacular service that trickles meanly back along the ceiling and the wall behind, where one can never get a fair swipe at it.

Even now, the Doctor did not notice Van der Valk, though that gentleman put himself more and more impudently in full view. The "heavy mob" went for a swim in the pool, which was kept a whole hour for them on "their" evening, reappeared beautifully dressed for a ceremonious whiskey at the bar, and left soon afterward, Dr. Post still unconscious, apparently, of the police presence that had been drinking whiskey at his very elbow.

Dr. Post was also a concertgoer. Van der Valk found himself at five concerts in two weeks on this account. He knew very little about music, except from Arlette's phonograph, and her taste was personal and cranky. She had a tendency to dislike all sopranos. He now enjoyed himself very much, discovered Bruckner, and was very taken with a Hungarian whose name he could not remember and who conducted the Eighth Symphony of Dvořák, which Van der Valk was delighted with. When he told Arlette about it, she was typically superior about "Czech folklore," and he was indignant. There was, too, a wonderful American Negro woman who did a Schumann group, a pretentious visiting conductor who conducted a messy Mozart and was applauded furiously for it (to the disgust, Van der Valk was glad to see, of Dr. Post, alone and austere among the *abonnés*), and a splendid German woman, quiet and gentle-looking, who played the violin with such love that he became quite converted to Bach sonatas he had always thought of as very dull.

Van der Valk did not think there was anything puritanical about the Doctor. The lecherous puritan is a common enough phenomenon in Holland, but Post was more complex. He was a lover of sensuous delights, of civilized and luxurious arts, of pure pleasure. And Post was a collector of women the way he might have been of Sèvres china. Mrs. Merckel was not the only one; Van der Valk would venture a little bet on that.

Mrs. Beatrix van der Post had some connection with it, he felt. Van der Valk had seen her by now. Meditating on the luscious summer evenings under the lindens, he had had plenty of chances to study Madam. For the movements of both Posts were predictable, since they belonged to the chauffeured stratum of society. This chauffeur was not the figure of parody that stands stiffly saluting outside the marble portal of a Rolls-Royce; he brought the Alfa Romeo around to the front on evenings when Dr. Post was going out—and drove it, too, for Post either could not drive or disliked driving. And he brought Madam's little auto around every evening, because she always went out. It was a trim white BMW, a pretty little object, and she fitted into it like one of her elegant long white gloves. She had a trick of standing by it while surveying her house and herself with satisfaction before climbing in, which she did well, with no display of stockings.

Trim was the word for her. She had a solid Dutch figure, but she appeared slim in her excellent choice of clothes. A neatly rounded body, by no means unattractive, a keen, intelligent face with a high forehead

112

and a sharp nose a scrap too big but well-shaped, strong neat legs unbowed or bulged, with clean ankles and long shinbones.

Yet Van der Valk had no difficulty in seeing just what Cabestan had meant. Or why the girl Suzanne had never felt quite happy with this friendly, pleasant, kind woman. Or why Dr. Post had no great interest in pictures. The art whore, he suspected, looked at everything with the same self-satisfaction, with the same superiority. Her house, her clothes, her excellently composed body and ordered mind, her gleaming auto and gleaming driving style—she was an excellent driver. And her picture, her television program: and, of course, her artist and her producer. Everything she touched she would manage and arrange—and always so extremely well. . . .

Once or twice, for the hell of it, Van der Valk followed at a discreet distance and watched her getting out of the little white car as gracefully as she got in. What would that be like in bed? he wondered. He drew himself pictures of her undressing, but they were not erotic pictures. Mrs. Beatrix van der Post-Rouwé was not an erotic woman.

It didn't do to draw conclusions from such things, but Van der Valk was indeed making pictures—or, more accurately, tentative nervous scribbles—during these evenings. Post was plainly a not uncommon kind of person: the classic high-nervous type that likes and needs a quiet simple existence. Regular food, regular exercise, a lot of sleep. Such men have no great sexual capacity; Van der Valk thought that the Doctor's collection of women was more likely to be

113

imaginary than real. Perhaps such men have a feeling of suspected inadequacy, no?

Do not draw conclusions, Van der Valk thought. But the man was rather like Casimir, wasn't he? That same air of promise that has come to little. Had he looked at the other man, and seen a vision that was like his own future, and rather hated it?

How would he react, Van der Valk asked himself suddenly, if I were to invite him to meet me personally? For a game of squash, say? Get away from being policeman and doctor. In that consulting room I'll never reach him; he's too armored. But on my ground —outside?

Suppose I were to point out this similarity to him, over a drink or something. The withdrawal from the world, the observation from a high vantage point, the need for girls and reliance on them—for wasn't that the one real contact with life they both had?

Might it stir him up?

There was nothing else Van der Valk could do. Dr. Post was sitting pretty. All he had to do was stay quiet another week and Van der Valk would have made a brief, impersonal report to Mr. Samson that there was nothing to be done. A formally worded little letter would have gone off to Mr. Merckel. And that would be that.

He gave Dr. Post a telephone call, and extended his invitation. And was surprised. He thought it would be refused politely. It was accepted. What ailed the fellow?

PART TWO

1

WHY HAVE I CHOSEN to write this, to put it all on paper—even, on occasion, to write my own words in dialogue form? I could call it an exercise in detachment, a formal method for studying the chain of circumstance. There are no grounds for doing so. I have the requisite objectivity and do not need to go to such pains in order to reassure myself. Nor is this a casebook for others. I have no desire for immortality as a book in the dusty clinical files of the Faculty Library, to be used for the edification of dim students.

But perhaps for one pair of eyes? Can I trust him? I can, I believe, for even if his blessed regulations compel him to communicate all such findings to the legal authorities, he will not do that, if I have understood him. He is capable of illegality—as I am.

I will emphasize that this is a dialogue. Or I should

say, rather, a conversation between us. You see, I can address you directly, now that I have decided. If you read these pages, it will be because you have understood, and will be capable of understanding better. That is why I have put in fragments of conversations that have passed between us. Listen to my words again, and put them together with the words I have added. I have said, "If you ever read this." That will be when you have obtained formal proof against me. You will have realized, at the same time, that formal proof was not enough. For lawyers, yes, but not, I think, for you.

I am not a psychopath and have no compulsion to do dangerous things, to court risks, to bring about my own downfall. I have no hunger to confess, to be caught. You are trying to exert pressure upon me, but you have no lever of compulsion. No, it will be because you have built up patiently, step by step, a chain of circumstantial evidence. You will find it very difficult. (I am speaking of all this in the future tense still; it has not yet happened, after all. Perhaps it never will? No, I told you I possessed detachment. I have also courage, honesty, and the ability to resist self-deception. You will arrive.)

You will find it discouraging. But behind the mass of silence and deception, you will winkle out scraps of real evidence. It is there, after all, and it will point to me in the end.

To prove to you that I have foresight, that I am not even worried, I will show you that I have thought of everything. Full proof will be lacking, inevitably. You will construct a rigmarole of minor charges. I will have an expensive, skillful advocate, a lot of money, a great

116

deal of patience. I may not secure acquittal—and I do not greatly care if I do not, for I will not waste a lot of time. A year in prison, with time deducted for waiting to come to trial—and, of course, the full deduction for good behavior. I shall be very well behaved.

But then? After? That, you are thinking, will be the worst part. The disgrace, the broken career, the pointing finger, the whisper behind the fat soft knuckles. My dear fellow, not a bit. It would not alarm me to be deprived, even permanently, of my license to practice medicine. I am a good doctor. Nobody can take away my skill and experience. You wonder what I will do? I am a handy electrical craftsman, and quite complex gadgets are within my scope. I could find interesting and well-paid work. And, of course, in many countries I could simply set up as a quack. The word does not alarm me. I have known quacks of a great deal more use to their patients than most doctors that are officially recognized. Nor am I alarmed about social position, "standing."

But let us get back to our conversation. Our criminal conversation. The phrase amuses me. It is the kind of phrase I will find in the list of charges read against me. Is it a criminal charge, or only a civil one? Does it even still exist on the statute book? I hope so; I find it amusing. There will be other trifling things, no doubt. Illegal possession of drugs not accounted for, or some other tedious and labored phrase.

This conversation of ours will never be mentioned in any court. In reading it, you will have observed that you cannot show it to anyone without compromising yourself and your career, which is no doubt precious to you. You will not hold this against me, if you are the man I take you for. You are given to unguarded remarks, Mr. van der Valk. Even indiscreet. The kind of thing that journalists call "off the cuff." All journalists, of course, cling like limpets to the coarse cliché, but have you noticed how old-fashioned journalese often sounds? Who, in the last thirty years, has worn starched cuffs?

This will make a bulky manuscript. You will get practice in deciphering my handwriting, with its scribbles and its jumps, its clarity and precision, and the personal abbreviations all doctors use. We are accustomed from our earliest student days to large quantities of notes, which to be any use at all must be full, clear, and perfectly comprehensible, however much haste was used in taking them down. It is no hardship for me to write at this length. When I was a student, my notes were constantly borrowed by the others. Every night I wrote them up religiously from the day's scratch-paper roughs into a series of big loose-leaf volumes. It was my greatest pleasure in student days. How I loved—and still do—a large new loose-leaf notebook! With what pleasure I watched it fill! There, if you like, is one of the answers to your question—why all this? It is a pleasure.

I know what you will say, of course. You will say (it is one of the axioms at the police school, no doubt), "The characteristic, overriding, never-failing mark of the criminal, by which he can always be recognized, is his immense vanity."

Very likely they are right. And has a writer, too, no vanity? Are not all his characters reflections of himself? Are not his books a measure of his exhibition-

118

ism? You have yourself, my dear Van der Valk, considerable vanity.

So here I am now, an hour's work or more already, scribbling away happily. It will all have quite a smell of M. Simenon. Yes indeed, I read him, too; so do you, no doubt. Don't we all? The man, of course, is simply a good doctor. Indeed, his nostalgia for his other vocation shows through constantly. But I am not copying his technique, though I recall a book of his presenting a similar situation. You recall *Letter to My Judge?* By a doctor! But there is no resemblance, I am afraid, between M. Simenon's imaginary awkward rustic in a French provincial town and my very real self—from a quite aristocratic background—in the city of Amsterdam.

I recall the book very well. It was an appeal, for the man had been tried and condemned; nobody had understood and he could not bear that. He chose as the object of his letter the only man who, he thought, had made a serious effort to comprehend—the judge who had drawn up the instruction in his case.

You see how the parallel fails? You cannot, my dear chap, see me doing that. *Pas si bête.* As for understanding—everything, not just barely enough—I don't care a damn whether you do or not. I'm not appealing to you. Understand *that,* at least.

2

I paused at that last sentence, I remember (this is a day or so later), for I found myself slipping into a sort of meditation about the kind of life I would lead on my release from prison. I shall be able to make a good

119

living, I have told you. I shall keep up my studies in prison, and develop my knowledge of electronics. They are so humane and conscientious, and, of course, bothered by having educated men as their guests; they will certainly give me every opportunity for study. But my private life? You have seen me, always known me, in this large, luxuriously fitted and furnished house. A solid and comfortable house. I am surrounded by comforts, stuffed with bourgeois ornament, including my dear wife. Well, my friend, I shall whisper a little secret to you. You recall my mentioning the psychopath's longing to be caught, to confess? And my assured denial that such was not my case? Aha, you thought. No no, my friend, I shall be quite glad to be caught, but only because it is the one really secure way—short of killing her, of course—of getting rid of my dear wife. I do not think I would be able to kill her. She would, I am afraid, catch me out in the attempt.

But the comfort of my life—will you be surprised to hear that I am well able to part with all that? Didn't I say that I was detached? And I interpret the word in its strict sense. I do not hold fast to any material thing. I enjoy them often, but I have a very loose hold on my possessions, my encumbrances. I have for a long time hankered for the life again of a student, living alone in a single room, simply furnished. I shall be one of those elderly bachelors, cooking my meals on a gas ring and reading while I eat. Indeed, to read while I eat, alone, in leisure, with no damned table talk, has always been one of my dearly loved pleasures. Another has been to sit, while everybody was dashing about accompanied by bustle and noise, in a dim, quiet room, listening to the rain out-

side the window—or on the zinc roof over the window
—beating, trickling. That is pleasure for you. I shall
have a life, in fact, similar to Cabestan's—or, rather, to
that which he could have had with any sense.

Yes, I killed him. And you will say (no, you will not,
perhaps, but the prosecutor will), "What sort of doctor
is this, Mr. President, who showed such callous, elementary disregard for human life?"

The answer will become apparent to you—if it has
not already.

He should not, of course, have tried to blackmail
me. That was treading on a banana skin: then he ran
out of time extremely suddenly. Ill on Thursday,
worse on Friday, died on Saturday. Solomon Grundy
would have been a good name for Cabestan.

I shall not bother you, my dear Van der Valk, with
a technical description. There are so many ways a doctor can cause death with no pain, leaving no trace. He
did not suffer. I am reminded of a ridiculous English
criminal process—do you recall that rather pathetic
doctor, who resembled a figment of M. Simenon's
imagination a good deal more than I do, who was accused of murdering an ancient widow with overdoses
of heroin? She was in even worse shape than Cabestan, for she was bedridden and practically gaga.
The idea was of such stupidity, such clumsiness, such
a waste of time—shall we say as much of all three as
the trial itself?

3

I must not lose coherence, and I must avoid all suggestion of a long rambling monologue attempting

self-justification. I must put everything in order for the eye of an "orderly policeman." And I must give you a frame of reference. As I promised, I am going to reproduce fragments of our dialogue, which will help you. My memory is trained and retentive, and I took rough notes immediately each time you left me. If you have notes yourself, compare them with this record, and if there is any discrepancy, it is your notes, my friend, that are dishonest. You will see with surprise that I have reproduced your words accurately. Your words! I have even caught your speech rhythm and your verbal mannerisms.

We are going to go back now, as a starting point, to the day you first came—what word shall I choose? On the whole, "breezing in" does not convey it badly. Not too aggressive, not too confident, quite nicely mannered, and intelligent enough to be provoking if not alarming. And oh, so very tactful! All your impudence, even the supreme impudence of having yourself announced as a patient, was presented, impudently, as "tact." I enjoyed you at once. You were watchful, too—a very patient patient.

I am sitting now as I write in my consulting room, at my desk, exactly as I was then. To my left is the hall, where patients enter and leave, never seeing one another, for that upsets them. You need see nothing sinister in that; any psychiatrist does the same. Facing me across the room are the doors to my examination rooms, where I keep the electrical machinery that intrigues you, and to the famous bathroom.

You walked in with a solid step (although you are fairly light on your feet for a biggish man), which I have learned since to recognize. I could see at a glance

122

that you were no patient. What you were took me longer to grasp, yes, but I knew before you told me.

"Good afternoon. Tell me how I can be of service to you."

You began at once with one of your crude jokes. "My nerves are all right, Doctor, but I do need to be sure I'm not imagining things. I'm in search of the same things as most people—truth, knowledge, reassurance."

"I see. You wish to be reassured, you want knowledge, and you ask for truth. Those things, as you say, are common to most people's wishes. Have you anything more precise to tell me? You suspect that you imagine things. Do you hear things? See them? Feel them? But we had better start at the beginning." I took out one of my case-history sheets.

"Your name?"

"Van der Valk, Peter."

"And you are how old?"

"Thirty-eight."

"And your occupation is?"

"Inspector of police, recherche department."

I was, of course, far too well under control to make any reaction you might have hoped for. "Make yourself comfortable. We have plenty of time; all my initial appointments are for an hour. Smoke if you feel like it. I am going to ask you a few questions to give me the feeling of your trouble."

"Sure," you said amiably. You brought out a rather sat-on blue package of Gitane ciarettes; you offered me one in a friendly way, which I took.

"Yes, I'll keep you company. A doctor, you know, must not seem chilly or disdainful."

"You establish the rapport," you said.

"Pretentious phrase. I'm not a psychiatrist, you know. If I can help you, it will be in a tangible, actual way. Purely mental disturbances are not in my line, but we will see. You have interesting work. At times trying? Irregular hours? A shortage of sleep, sometimes? Interruption of your home life? You are occasionally overtired?"

"That sounds like a doctor," you said. "Well, I am a doctor, too, in a way. All that is true but I have no complaints about it. Part of life."

"Excellent. So you feel equal to the demands of your work in general. And you have no unusual fears or worries, or a feeling of being inadequate?" I asked.

"I'll just have to tell you the details." You had realized that I was fencing with you. "About what is worrying me, as precisely as I can."

"I am listening attentively."

"By virtue of your profession, you're a very discreet man. And so am I. We have a lot in common. Both nerve specialists, you might say. You might agree that most of your work is palliative, not much more. Mine, too." You had decided to match the glossy joviality of my manner. I was still amused by you.

"I had never guessed that a police officer would one day call on me in this way," I said, perhaps maliciously.

"That is the point. I haven't come as a police officer in the ordinary way, ringing loudly at the bell with big boots on, giving the girl at the door something to gossip about, embarrassing you from the start. I would like you to appreciate that point. I preferred to try to create a personal, confidential, amicable atmosphere.

124

Nobody likes the police in his house. I say no more than the truth when I say that I come in much the same spirit as a patient. I am slightly worried, a good deal puzzled, and I hope for your help."

"But, my dear Mr. van der Valk, you are aware that my consulting time is quite an expensive item. Or are you proposing that I send an account in to the Department of Justice?"

"Why not?" you said, amused by the idea. "Might do them good. They send accounts in to people—demand immediate payment, what's more." I admired your parry and riposte, but you had decided to stop the double talk; it was getting you nowhere.

"Come, Doctor," you said, more seriously. "You mustn't be averse to my trying to throw no shadow on your life. I am a reasonable person, and I won't be taking up much of your time."

"I find your approach most sympathetic, but I'm bound to say that I'm quite in the dark still. What is it I can do to help?"

"The approach"—you were trying now to stretch my nerves by making me wait for it—"was deliberate. Naturally, since I have come as a private person I have no official standing. You could, of course, refuse to speak to me, be pompous or frigid, stand on your dignity. I am hoping that you will meet me halfway, and speak freely."

I wondered whether I was supposed to react to this as to a blackmail effort. It was certainly intended to give that impression. Under that sunny, talkative manner of yours, you are fond of this type of little trap. I did not, of course, fall into it. I leaned back and crossed my legs, and blew smoke across the space between us.

"There are various answers to that," I said. "First, I am never pompous or frigid, I hope, with anyone, not even the eccentric, the absurd-sounding, the unbalanced-seeming. I have heard tales far more confused and peculiar than yours; they are a professional commonplace. I might add that my reaction of patience is also professional. I have my human share of impatience with meandering tales of imaginary ills and grievances that waste a doctor's day.

"Second, I never throw anybody out. I used to have a man who made endless threats to kill me. Finally, one day, he shot at me across the street when I was getting into my car. He'd been released two or three times from psychiatric institutions—the relatives claimed he was quite harmless. I got him fixed up in the end.

"Third, I'm not in the least bothered by policemen; they are just like any other people—no lesser, no greater tendency toward neurosis."

Yes, I knew I was talking too much. But I had, you see, to fortify my whole position against the stroke I knew was coming. "Lastly, your tale may be interesting or it may be foolish; I haven't heard it yet. But I will listen attentively, Mr. van der Valk. You are, as you tell me, a police officer, and I imagine that this most involved approach of yours has some relation to a crime. Some accusation, no doubt. You find me too quick to protest? I am in a very sensitive profession, and we live in a very sensible land. There are people who feel that a doctor has not listened with sufficient sympathy to tales of self-pity, or who

126

feel that he is insufficiently lenient toward self-indulgence in alcohol, perhaps, or drugs. What do you suppose is my reaction toward people who come—as they do come, I assure you—to solicit me for narcotics? These people direct their unbalanced resentments at the physician. They make little plots and denunciations, they spread malicious inventions—they are quite safe from pursuit, since what is it but trivial gossip? The physician learns to protect himself against such. No, my friend, nothing you may have to say to me could shock me."

"You won't be surprised, then,"—I had left you no way out now—"to hear that you have been accused of murder."

"Not particularly. I am not a surgeon, thank heaven. It happens to them daily. And, of course, there still persists the old superstition that anesthetists are no better than a brood of poisoners. But I haven't had a patient die suddenly in years."

"Not murdered by negligence, Dr. Post. Nor of a patient. You are accused of willful homicide of a person known to you. A certain Cabestan."

"Old Cabestan, really? How remarkable. But I can't think who would wish to blame me for his death, poor old chap."

"It's even stronger. You are accused of bringing his death about, of your own active agency, by hitherto undetermined means."

"Now, that does astonish me, really. I had thought it probable that he had picked up a dose of pneumonia or some such thing that carried him off. He was fairly elderly, somewhat frail, lived alone—such a death, even when sudden, is never very surprising."

We were fencing again. I am not going on; that is enough to remind you how our first conversation went. It was inconclusive. I did not ask you how you had received the accusation, nor who had made it. I had, to begin with, a notion that you wouldn't tell me. But principally my whole attitude had to be that of smiling indifference, to murder or anything else. The world is full of people who make accusations. Policemen at your level get hundreds. I decided that you had told the truth. Accusations have to be checked; you had come, politely, tactfully, as you claimed, to do some checking. I found that natural. You would not, I thought, come again.

But after you left, with a few jokes I found rather overpolished through long usage, I found myself wondering. You were too amused, you made too many jokes. A policeman in your position would be excessively stiff and embarrassed in conversation with a person as well known and highly regarded in his profession as I am. You were not stiff enough. You looked, too, as much as you talked—at myself, at my surroundings, at everything—and you are, you will be the first to admit, an expansive talker. I did not find much reassurance in your eye.

4

I had, of course, considered the fact that Casimir might have had some confidant. But this confidant could be nobody that the police—or anyone else—would think of as a reliable witness, because the confidence would disclose the fact that Casimir was attempting blackmail. I say attempting because, of course, he never got a penny from me. I do not understand the mentality of anyone who pays blackmail. One knows it will never stop. However great the cowardice of the blackmailed persons, the sensation of being skinned at regular intervals must grow too strong. There will come a time sooner or later to all of them when killing is easier than paying. But if everybody thought like that, there would be no blackmailers, either. The life expectancy would be too short.

There is another possibility. Casimir may have tried this game on another person, or even several. If those persons had an inkling that I was proposed for entry to their club, they might have drawn conclusions from Casimir's demise and pitched in some accusation—anonymously, of course—to divert any eventual suspicion from themselves. But I did not think much of this notion. I have never put your intelligence so low, my friend, as to imagine that a responsible officer of police would entertain an anonymous denunciation of an utterly respectable doctor. In order to approach me at all, however tactfully or obliquely, the police had, I knew, something a good deal stronger. Some live, real, actual person.

Casimir I inherited when I took over this house from old Dr. Munck, who retired—still enormously active, full of years, honors, and wealth—at the age of nearly eighty and went immediately on a walking holiday at some winter-sports center, where he was obstinate enough to disregard local knowledge and was killed the next day by a fall of loose snow. Casimir's tenancy came about, I should guess, some time in the thirties. The supply of country girls began to dry up; servants had grown too dear and too bad. Munck had the servants' story simply chopped on, and he made a thorough job of it; builders, at least, had not yet grown too dear. For it was a drastic job and crude, if effective. A staircase running down the whole side of the house, and a street door built in at the corner! Nobody would do such a thing now. But it was quite common then in houses where all the rooms were too big and all the houses were too tall— and not a one of them with an elevator!

Casimir's tenancy was never the slightest drawback. As the house stood, it was quite big enough for a childless couple as well as a busy practice. Casimir never had the slightest contact with my house or myself; there was no need. And old Munck had been quite content with the tiny rent it brought in, and so was I. As for Casimir, he had had more sense than ever to complain about his three flights of steep narrow stairs. A real studio flat in Amsterdam is the rarest species of game in Holland.

I was under no compulsion, naturally, to tell anyone that I had been in Casimir's quarters. I made, and make, no secret of the fact that I have keys to his doors. Why should I? It is normal because of fire; a special clause in the policies covers that flat. There are, moreover, plumbing fixtures, electric wiring, and so on. If a pipe burst or something similar happened, I had to be able to let the workmen in. As it is, on the very rare occasions when something has happened, I gave instructions that the workmen were to go and bother Casimir. I am a doctor, after all, busy and harassed, in the eye of most people an important personage. Even in his best days, Casimir was never any more than a down-at-the-heels painter, a person plainly born to be bothered by plumbers.

Then, when a polite letter told me that he had trouble with a leaking roof, I went to see about it, like a good careful landlord. I had become a little curious about Casimir, and the pretext was handy; a couple of tiles needed replacing. I think the episode increased his curiosity about me; it certainly increased mine about him. I had scarcely been aware of his existence. The house is almost noiseless and he was a mouse-like fellow, not given to weight lifting, tap dancing, or manipulating pneumatic drills.

Up and up I had to go, along that interminable stairway covered in some sort of cocos matting, mud-colored long since. It smelled bad; I have an extremely sensitive nose. The rent was low—but not too low, I thought while climbing.

There is a sort of hallway at the top, with various cupboards full of brooms and things, wastebaskets and electricity meters and ancient overcoats—I have looked since, you see. A short passage, and at the end a door to a kind of glory hole—decaying trunks filled with junk, and the plumbing pipes. On the landing were four doors, for there had been three servants' bedrooms, and a bathroom. The bathroom is now half kitchen, and two contiguous rooms have been knocked into one big studio, with mansard windows at the front of the house. There was water, gas, and electricity. It must be a pretty good apartment for a painter. I know little of such things, but he was high, quiet, well lit, secure from interruption, and he possessed several roof and street scapes. As well as fine opportunities for studying typists changing their frocks in a building opposite, between two of the lindens; sure enough, when later on I hunted about a little, a pair of cheap binoculars was among the first things I found.

Casimir was waiting for me on the landing. He was a tall scraggy thin, very round-shouldered, wearing, as always, a baggy hairy-tweed suit of old-fashioned cut, with flappy trousers and padded shoulders to make him more impressive, which it didn't. He had had red hair, now gone gray. His big head and big anxious wrinkled forehead gave him a superficially impressive look. He had horn-rimmed glasses pushed down on his nose, an eternal cigarette between his flabby lips and his disgusting teeth; I would have been ready to hate him on account of his breath alone. If he had been put out in the sun and wind of Provence, well dried out, disinfected, and browned, he would have been less revolting. He had a moist pasty look, and his scurfy scalp from above that skull of a face was really degrading. Can you accept that a young girl finds that attractive?

I am told that he was a good painter in his day, and had even produced memorable work and been world-famous in the twenties. But he had outlived his talents, and he lived, I am told, through the years following the war on a steadily declining reputation, though his name still sufficed to find a market for his work. No, my authority for all this is not, as you might think, my dear wife. Apart from the fact that I have scant regard for her much-vaunted artistic judgment, I know that she strongly disliked Casimir and that the feeling was returned. She once, it seems, made a cutting remark about some work of his in his hearing. . . . No, I know a surgeon, with whom I play squash, who collects modern paintings, and he has a picture done by Casimir around 1930 that he says has real worth. Casimir had been a prodigious worker once and was still—here my authority is someone who knew him closely—capable of bouts of astonishing activity between the weeks of nothing but gin.

Certainly his name, even before I began inquiring about him, meant something to me, but there is nothing dimmer than a figure that had a great success in the twenties. One thinks, Good heavens, is he still alive?

The flat smelled worse even than the stairs, though very likely an ordinary person would have noticed nothing. It was untidy only in some places, and seemed on the whole to be kept clean. I listened to his mumbling voice, had the patches of damp on his ceiling pointed out, and agreed to get the roof repaired with no more ado.

I think that I meant to kill him even then.

5

I thought about that flat in the days following. Would it not have been a better—and more suitable—place for me to have chosen to live in than this pork pie of a house, stuffed with the expensive trappings of thick carpets, rich curtains, and a fur-coated wife? (I nearly said fur-coated tongue, for that is the taste this house gives me.) Was it not an evil chance that I should have become a doctor, forced to keep up an elaborate front, and not a painter, who can keep up a front or not exactly as he pleases? Naked women are as much a salient feature of his life as they are of a doctor's; nobody would have fastened spitefully upon my perfectly harmless activities. There is no Medical Association with a censorious eye upon what a painter does or says. He is even expected to behave in a peculiar way, and if he should happen to be detected in some scabrous activity, there will be a rush of sympathizers —there has been, no doubt, a reaction in favor of Cabestan, now that he is dead—all blithely declaring that not only is lechery quite normal to an "artist" but an integral part of him, necessary to him. I have heard Beatrix on this subject. Broad-minded, tolerant as she would never be to those she regards as "her class of people," she prated that lechery is a fertilizer in which the flowers of art reach their splendor. "Art is a flower," she pontificates. "You don't grow flowers in a marble quarry." Bitch . . .

Am I not an artist, too? Why not? Why should there be a barrier in the minds of the ignorant between science and the arts? Life is organic, a whole. It is these barriers, splitting and sealing off, that stunt, stultify, desiccate the cheese nibblers like my wife and her precious friends.

"Aha," you will say, upon reading this paragraph, "he's jealous." Yes, jealous. I killed that wretched Casimir out of personal, professional—animal—jealous hatred. That bastard stole my life. When he blackmailed me, it was to me a thin shadow of formal excuse. For the blackmail itself I cared not a rap. Bella has a husband well able to look after her.

134

6

I got so heated that I stood up and walked about. Then I went and had a look at myself in the bathroom looking glass. (Bella says she has never been better-looking in any mirror than in this one.) I do not look at myself for your benefit, my dear Van der Valk. I am aware that your trained eye has absorbed every detail of my appearance and manner that could appear indicative. I do the same. Like me, you accustom yourself to using meetings, conversations, examinations as tools in your trade. We have, as you have remarked jokingly on two or three occasions, a great deal in common. . . . You form impressions of people. Is So-and-So likely to be a criminal? No, that is not fair to you. Is he capable of being criminal? I would say—and, for all I know, you would agree with me—that everybody is. Regardless of who or what he may be.

No, I went to look in the glass above the washstand to look at the man as you see him. I wish to see what you see. I am not even familiar with my own appearance, for I have no personal vanity and except as attributes to love I dislike looking glasses. I shave with my jaw reflected in the tiny mirror set into the inside of my razor box. I comb my hair, which is short and straight, without needing any reference to my reflection. I know that it is clean, tidy, and healthy; what further interest have I? At the barbers', I keep my eyes resolutely shut; I find it a good place to rest, and it discourages their infernal tattle. In my apartment, I have no looking glasses; I pay large amounts of money to tailors to see that my suits fit me. The only glass there is in any room I frequent is the one above the washstand, in the bathroom between the examination and the consulting rooms.

It is one of the most important places in the house! How many women who arrived in my house combed and collected, impeccably painted, sometimes cold and haughty to cover their fear, have later seen themselves disheveled in that glass! It excited and fascinated you from the start, I noticed. You need no guiding hand through that labyrinth at least. One of the first things you did, I'll be bound, was to make a little sketch map of the way the house is arranged. Old Munck, of course, had this consulting room, and his examination room at the back, as it is now, the discreetly curtained windows of the former veranda looking out at the chestnut tree in the garden. But Munck had his secretary in the "bathroom," and his waiting room was the one opening off the hall. It was my idea to put my secretary upstairs and have a second waiting room there. It greatly annoyed Beatrix, but it was quite natural and not in the least sinister. A neurologist is always half psychiatrist, and patients do not care to meet each other or to be seen by anyone but myself and Miss Maas—and not always by her. By no means always! She leaves at four-thirty, and her day is taken up with the telephone and the appointments book, the records and the accounts. My most solid witness! She has been with me since I began in practice, and never has seen anything not of the most perfect propriety. Nor, I may add, would she believe it if she did. She has known patients to behave in the oddest ways and nothing surprises her. You will have decided, regretfully, that Miss Maas will be of little use to you.

But we were talking about the bathroom. I admit that it is vulgar. There are heavy rubber tiles that have a pleasantly soft mat feel under bare feet. The washstand and the bidet are *"porcelaine de Paris,"* with the classic ivy-leaf motifs, and the shower is lined with tiles in the same pattern. The towel rail is heated, and there is discreet austere soap from Roger & Gallet. I do admit that any expensive hotel gives you just the same. That is the point, in a sense, as you will see if you think a moment.

For you wrinkled your nose at it. You found this luxury contemptible, and though you said nothing, your face told me that in Holland the most expensive doctors content themselves with a plain washstand in the corner of the examination room, and that this was all very singular and suspect.

You make me laugh, because for all your sophisticated experience you are a puritan still. Even here in Amsterdam, the only town in Holland where there is a scrap of aristocracy and a scrap, as well, of canaille, one can never be outside the sphere of conventional morality. To have a bath more than once a week is simply not done. As far as I know, I am the only person who has succeeded in breaking that rule.

I am making excuses. I know that the bathroom is a weakness, and not only in the evidential sense. It is my streak of sensuality and my yielding, for once, to the power of sheer wealth. And the women enjoy it so! In my bathroom, a woman puts back her face, her self-command—her mask of morality! After a half hour in my bathroom, no woman has ever shown the

137

faintest sign of hysteria, of rancor, of jealousy, or of any emotional exaggerations. It is a therapy—just like everything else I do. I always left them there for as long as they wished. When they came out, I would be writing quietly at my desk. But I had nearly forgotten, in the defense of my bathroom, that I went there to have a look at myself, wondering what you will find, there behind the features.

The features are nothing remarkable. My hair is short and straight, and is combed to the side at the top of a fairly high forehead. The face is long and narrow, with large ears and a wide mouth. The eyes and nose are large, too, but regular. No, the face is not bad, I confess; it has character and humor as well as intelligence. Nobody will believe there should be malice in the lines I have around eyes and mouth, and nobody will think that the character in that straight nose and neat jaw can be so very dreadful. My voice is deep, calm, and deliberate, with quite a pleasant intonation, and the eyes are clear gray and have a level frank look. As a doctor, this face has helped me a good deal. With women, of course, a face is unimportant. I could have the face of an orangutang, the wild man of the woods, and it would never have made the faintest odds. What is it you see? I am curious.

7

You appeared again a week and more after the first time. I suppose you had calculated that this was a good interval, enough to make me stew tender, grow uneasy, begin to crumble. I had not crumbled, because I know how people like you work. I had decided that you were anything but satisfied, and that unsatisfied you would be like a bulldog. I knew that while you would find little to grip in my slippery surface, it would be a long while before you let go. There would be a long period of patient calm enforced upon me before you went away, satisfied or not.

This time again, I was struck by a certain force of imagination you possess. You had thought up an original comic approach that was designed to put me off my stroke, and you would, I guessed, continue this tip-and-run act, a war of irritation and attrition. I felt fairly sure that you would never adopt the laborious plodding of the average police action, setting large men in raincoats to watch the house, with long tedious lists of every visitor. You wanted to gain a foothold in my castle, among my fortifications, there to build a subterranean sap to blow me up when I least expected it. So you phoned Miss Maas for an appointment exactly like any businessman with symptoms, and in you sailed to the consulting room, cheerful and full of obtuse self-satisfaction. I was not deceived by this air of imbecility.

"Would you prefer the chair there, or do you feel more at ease on the sofa?"

My consulting room is extremely pleasant, a large high square room with two big windows that face the tree-shaded street. It was fine warm weather and all the lindens were looking their best. My desk is placed on a slant, between the windows and the side wall, lined with bookshelves, behind which one goes zigzagging upstairs toward Casimir. There is no more furniture than is needed in this room, but there is a large sofa of warm yellowish leather. Plenty of people, and especially women, prefer to sit there than in the "customer's" chair at the corner of my desk.

"I think I do prefer the sofa," you said, in your voice of jovial idiocy. "I like the look of it very much."

"How's your health?"

"I don't know; there's all sorts of queer things wrong with me, I suspect. What can you treat?"

"Many things. Not conditions plainly requiring surgery, though I have sometimes succeeded in avoiding it even when it looked urgent."

"But there is a thing called neurosurgery."

"A very exacting discipline, outside my abilities. I could probably whip your appendix out for you; that's just elementary carpentry."

"What do you do most of?" you asked.

"I get a lot of people whose troubles border on the psychiatric and who need no psychiatric treatment. And, of course, many people on the obverse side, with insomnia or something that they imagine is a sign of mental trouble, due to a purely physical origin. And, evidently, an army of psychosomatic aches and pains. Is that what you want to know?" I asked.

"You do massage?"

"Frequently. And I often send patients to a masseur."

"And electric things, shock and so on?"

"I give no shock treatments; they belong in certain types of insanity. I use vibration, warmth, sometimes heat, various short waves, ranging from ultraviolet to feeble X ray. I also use warm air and both warm and cold water," I added, a little too sarcastically.

"And I suppose fruit and herb cures, and swimming, and riding bicycles?"

"Certainly. We have not, I'm afraid, the time to indulge in an explanation of the various possible applications of these things. You could, of course, go and read up your *Larousse Medical*."

"Oh, I have!" you shouted enthusiastically. "It's become my favorite reading these last weeks. You treat skin diseases?" you asked suddenly.

"I'm not a dermatologist. Occasionally I do. When they are of nervous origin, as they quite frequently are."

"And cosmetic treatments?"

I decided you needed a snub. "What are cosmetic treatments?"

"Oh, making old women beautiful again with calves' liver or some such thing."

"My poor friend, you have been reading magazines. There are cosmetic surgeons, and there are gerontologists, who use hormone treatments upon occasion. That is of no interest to me."

"I have been told you made people younger."

"Let me make myself clear. If a patient comes to me with a disordered system, living an overloaded or unhealthy life, and I am able to help him, he feels better. In a flush of well-being, he tells his friends he feels 'years younger,' and the ignorant, like you, loving drama, imagine that I possess magical powers and miracle cures. Superstition."

You were not too snubbed. During this absurd speech, you looked at me steadily, with your sunny, benevolent expression unchanged. "You have, however, a large number of women patients in early middle age."

"And do I really need to explain that to you?"

141

"Do. Why not? Since, as you say, I am ignorant."

"Every doctor has many patients of the type you describe. They are bored, nervous from doing nothing, needing distractions and amusements—a fertile ground for all sorts of ills. Add that women of this age suffer various biological disturbances and you get the common coin of every doctor's life. Why do we discuss these trivialities?"

"They may not be altogether trivial. They may even have a suspicion of malpractice about them."

I turned a glassy eye on you. "I have concluded that you have received some scurrilous letter. Accusing me of making off with old Cabestan and now, apparently, of malpractice with women patients—if I understand you rightly."

A casual nod from you.

"What I do not understand is your taking these rubbishy things seriously. A person with a grievance, exactly as I sketched for you at a previous meeting, often seizes upon anything that might be grounds on which a doctor could be attacked."

"We got one quite sober letter, not at all in scurrilous terms, simply saying that you had suppressed Cabestan because he had evidence that you misconducted professional relationships and had threatened to expose the fact." Your voice was colorless.

"Unfortunately," I said dryly, "Mr. Cabestan's death is the one fact that is real and demonstrable in all this. If you really feel that anyone, not to speak of myself, killed him, you surely need something to support the supposition. Was there any medical examination, for instance?"

"Oh, yes."

"With what result, if I may allow myself the curiosity of asking?"

"None whatever," you said cheerfully.

"Then surely the whole idea falls apart. This accusation could not stand up in a court. I hesitate to threaten, myself, but you must realize that any person accused on insufficient grounds of criminal action possesses means of defending himself. Wrongful arrest, interference with the liberty of the subject, or whatever."

"Has anybody interfered with your liberty?" you asked politely.

"Defamation of character."

"There isn't any. Come, Doctor, I'm your patient, and any conversation between us is private and privileged. The famous medical secret."

"A conversation sounding like blackmail?"

"We don't blackmail people," you said mildly. "Nor do we pursue frivolous accusations without grounds."

"You mean you really think you do have grounds?"

"Oh, yes. We even have a witness."

"Produce this witness."

"When the time comes," you said gently.

"A witness, my friend, that hides is not a very solid witness, nor is it one in whom anybody could have confidence. I think that I will ask my professional association to take steps to insure my protection. I will complain against illegal, unauthorized, and unjustifiable police interference."

You had been leading me on, of course, with deliberately weak arguments, tempting me to come out with this. I had been trapped, as I now realized. You proceeded now to blackmail me quite shamelessly.

143

You have, my dear Van der Valk, some good qualities, and you have, as well, a sort of low cunning that is revolting.

"You do that, Doctor," you said, with your country boy's broad smile, "if you really think it would do you any good to make any aspect of this affair more public. If you take such steps, the press gets the substance of the complaint against you; it's inevitable. You might end up by regretting your hasty move. As things stand, this is all no more than a friendly, discreet, personal little chat between you and me. Doctor and patient! This witness—we do not produce him simply because we wish to know how much weight to give his words. A standard of comparison. The person to provide that is you; surely that's obvious. You must realize that my movements are heavily biased on the side of your protection and the assumption of your complete innocence of all this. Surely that is how it should be," you said silkily. "If you prefer—really prefer—a noisy, public, clumsy inquiry, with your secretary, your patients, even your wife dragged into the dirty-minded stare of the public, well . . . There would be a cloud of gossip—exactly that malicious and stupid gossip you mentioned at our first meeting. By all means, if you prefer it, but I cannot see that it would help you."

It wasn't badly done. If I did not make an intelligent answer, it would look bad whichever alternative I chose. I reached for a cigarette and lit it.

"Listen carefully, Mr. van der Valk, to what I have to tell you."

You indicated jovially that you were all ears.

"I find your behavior deplorable—typical, I suppose, of the police. You threaten me with mysteries, and when I seek to protect myself, you threaten me with publicity. I refuse to be stampeded by this talk of accusations and witnesses, all the purest invention. I cannot see what you hope to gain by pestering me, and I cannot, apparently, stop you without further annoyance. Very well, do what you please; that is at least the smallest of these irritations. I allow you to talk to me since only by so doing can I convince you that you are wasting your time. If you wish to spend your days hanging about my house, you must decide for yourself. I will give thought to the problem of how a citizen in a sensitive profession can best shield himself from Jacks-in-office. If you wish to go any further than speaking to me, nosing in my books or my household, you must provide yourself with legal authority, which I will contest. I make myself clear?"

You got up, laughing. "Suits me. This remains between the two of us. Just a friendly chat from time to time. Doctor and patient!" You laid your hand on the doorknob. "Which of us is which, eh, Doctor?" You walked out convulsed with idiotic merriment; quietly I watched you go, smoking and sending a screen of smoke after you, not bothering to make a polite face.

Is this witness of yours a pure invention? Do you really dare me to complain? You know certainly that if I did, you would lose your job, since your approach to me is blatantly unethical and illegal. Consequently you are very sure. Sure of yourself, sure that I will not dare either an official investigation or the subsequent publicity. You are a good poker player. I cannot, of course, welcome a knock-down-and-drag-out case, since sooner or later someone would lose his head and yelp out matters sufficiently compromising to me. On the other hand, you cannot possibly prove I killed Casimir. Of that I am quite sure.

Who could this witness be? Someone you cannot le-ally use, since you are so coy about it?

Could it conceivably be Beatrix?

There is somebody, or you would not dare me so brashly to complain of your indefensible behavior. Somewhere you have an ace in the hole.

8

I had no patients the evening that Casimir came. It must have been coincidence, since he cannot possibly have known that. I think now that he was merely pushing forward a pawn, thinking that if I reacted, he would develop his offensive. I agreed to see him out of curiosity as much as anything. This man whom I hated, whom I feared, who had already had an un-foreseen effect upon my life—I was curious to try and understand better. I envied him, his life. Is it not ab-surd? Be that as it may, I had no evening engagement. No patient, no mistress, no concert. And we live in Amsterdam. There is no question, as there would be in a German city of this magnitude and importance, of saying, "Have we nothing to do? Come, let us go to the opera."

Beatrix was going out, of course. She goes out every night that she does not spend chattering with her peers here or staring at her television programs. What on earth is it that she does? She cultivates her intellectu-als, I suppose. She frequents all sorts of pretentious and hollow figures that whim brings into fashion—

so-called painters and writers, very probably the self-styled *"conférenciers"* and *"cabaretiers"* of the television. These excursions she calls "being in touch with the stream of modern thought." I have, naturally, long given up trying to show her that a flow of chatter may well be called a stream, but that it is neither modern nor thought.

I do not speak like that out of vanity. I have myself few pretensions at being intellectual, and none at all at being modern, even in my work. Any doctor will confirm for you that scientific research into the origins of disease and into new nostrums is sometimes impressive and occasionally heartening. He will also confirm that every lunatic asylum in Europe is filled to three times its maximum capacity.

As for thought . . . I am fairly widely read. By no means all my energies, whatever you may imagine, or my curiosities go into seducing women, an occupation that takes perhaps one per cent of my time. There are people who get more pleasure from the dodging and the plotting, the evasion of others and the making of furtive assignations, than they do from their rather pallid adulteries. I am not among them. My distraction is music. I go to perhaps half the concerts and recitals given here in Amsterdam, which are often very good.

You will have been puzzled to find that I appear to have no friends. It is true, but friendship is rare. I have a couple of professional friends, with whom I talk medicine or music. But I have a closed character. There is nobody who knows anything about me. There, my friend—believe me, I use the word here in consciousness of its meaning—you will have struck a blank. Make of the fact whatever you please.

I have, of course, a need for affection. You would be surprised to know how much I receive.

Casimir had written no note, of course. He rang at the front and I let him in myself. He had counted on my answering in person; he must know that I employ only daily help. There has never been a maid that slept in the house, and since Beatrix has always been sterile in every meaning of the word, there has never been a child to care for.

Casimir stood in the hallway gibbering and mouthing. Might he explain something? I supposed he was fussed about something the builders had said or done while mending the roof. I hoped they had not found dry rot; I am fond of this house and should be loath to see its fabric altered or replaced.

I let him into my consulting room. This is much more my private room than that idiotic "drawing room" Beatrix takes pride in, on the first floor. I have inherited all old Munck's arrangements, including the excellent idea that only patients should be allowed at the front door. He imagined the iron staircase at the back, and the glassed passage to the back door. The bell at the back rings in the kitchen during the day, and at night it is answered by the chauffeur—he prefers being called that to gardener—or his wife, in the cottage at the back. I have made no alterations at all, except for moving Miss Maas upstairs to make room for the "bathroom." One might think all this awkward, but things of this sort are inevitable when a doctor has his practice under his own roof, an arrangement I prefer to the English system of a house where four or five doctors hive together for consultation. There is no real invasion of privacy. Beatrix complains that since patients have been allowed upstairs they pretend to lose their way and peep at her rooms. I pay no attention; in anyone else's house she would do exactly the same. And if we do, by any chance, have guests, and as a consequence use the front door, the stairs, and the damned drawing room, it is evening and there are no patients. All European doctors have similar arrangements, and it is never a bother.

I sat Casimir down on the patient's chair, went myself to sit behind the desk, and held out the box of cigarettes to him, since for a wonder his mouth was empty. He took one greedily.

"Well. . . . Repairs gone off all right?" I asked. "No further trouble with the roof?"

"No . . . no. They replaced a few tiles, I think. I suppose you'll want to see exactly what they have done."

"I haven't the least interest in seeing what they have done." I may have sounded a scrap tart; Casimir looked flabbergasted, anyway. He is just the type to accuse the servants of theft if there were a rubber band missing. If he were as rich as Onassis, he would creep about from bathroom to bathroom sticking slivers of old soap together.

"What is it you wish to see me about?"

He shuffled about inside his tweed jacket, as though the hairs tickled his neck. "It's a—uh, personal matter, really."

I lit a cigarette myself, so that I would notice less the flavor of gin and unmended teeth that hung about.

"Since you asked especially to see me, I take it there is something on your mind."

"Yes indeed. Of importance. Just that . . . uh . . ." I

said nothing, looked at him. In all honesty, I had no suspicion whatever.

"The fact is that some time ago, one evening, I happened to be in the garden."

"And may I ask not only what you were doing in my garden but how you came to get into it?"

He surprised me by giving a pathetic answer—irrelevant, of course, but the truth, I think.

"I'm not getting any younger, and I find I get odd irrational fears, and I've been agitated at the idea that there might be a fire, and if I were upstairs and if I couldn't reach— If there were fire on the staircase, you see, and . . ." He just trailed off.

"Are you asking me to make you a fire escape or are you asking for advice about your irrational fears?"

"Well, yes, but that isn't really the most important."

"I'm afraid I won't consider the fire escape; if you find that flat too isolated, it would be best to look for another. What else is there, then?"

His answer was the really brazen remark of someone who is a great coward. "I have these fears, yes, but you see I'm getting on a bit, and I know of course I do drink a good deal, and I have worries about money, and I thought the best thing really would be if you could let me have a small regular sum of money."

Only then did light dawn. After all, I am a neurologist. People who come with the most rambling and incoherent tales of obscure fears are legion.

"Ah. And what do you think gives you a claim that regular sums of money would be the best treatment for your age and infirmities?"

Casimir, of course, had had this answer ready for a

long while. "What I saw in the garden," he said, with a decayed and sickly grin.

There are Venetian blinds covering the veranda windows where my examination room is built out, and there are curtains as well. How did anybody get into the garden, anyway, even at night, but by the aid of some involved and difficult clambering? Casimir has not what one would call an athletic figure, and I made up my mind at once that whatever he had seen or imagined, this was not a likely tale.

"Most remarkable," I said unpleasantly. "I am not a psychiatrist, Mr. Cabestan, but you might be well advised to try to realize how unreal this tale must sound. I can assure you that a practicing physician is not a honeypot for wasps to gather around."

He went red, patchily. "That high and mighty tone won't help you," he said, stung. "What I've got on you will make you sing smaller when it sinks in." He heaved his clotheshorse of a frame onto its feet and stumped jerkily toward the door.

"I'll give you twenty-four hours—no more—to think things over. After that—the Medical Association, and the press. I shouldn't wonder then if the police were quick to pay a call, too, once it was public. Twenty-four hours. I'll be at home. Just ring the doorbell when you've seen the light before this time tomorrow evening."

"Goodbye, Mr. Cabestan," I said politely. "Remember what I have said—a psychiatrist is more competent to help you than I am."

I watched him out, and observed him behind my curtains; he stood on the pavement awhile jerking around and mumbling to himself. When I heard the angry slam of his street door, which is only about three feet away, as you know, from my corner of the consulting room, I sat down to consider.

No, "consider" is the wrong word; that is pure self-deception. I was frightened and angry. It is frightening to discover someone has grounds for blackmailing one; the attempt itself gives a nasty nervous shock, and there is the added fear—an irksome nagging uncertainty—of not knowing what those grounds could be. What did he know—or, more exactly, how much? Just how much? With my belly full of fear, I thought at once about Suzanne. I had a good look at the garden, and then went back to the desk, where I poured out a moderate glass of cognac. I was a little calmer already. He could not have direct evidence. The most he could have was what he might conceivably have been told— the hows and the whys of the telling passed, for the moment, my understanding. Nobody would believe Cabestan. I did not think he was really mentally disturbed in any medical sense, but he was in poor health, vague, and unreliable—perhaps not exactly disreputable but not a figure to inspire confidence in anybody. "Except in young innocent girls," I muttered as wildly as he could have. My thoughts, nearly at peace, were turned suddenly to the overmastering hatred I felt for Casimir. One moment I was considering calmly that however damaging his insinuations were, no responsible person would believe him or give him audience; the next moment I was clutching the neck of the cognac bottle. I drank some then. It made me shudder violently, for I am not a drinker; I like a small glass before going to bed. Once again my thoughts stumbled, changed involuntarily, and took a new direction.

Casimir—I had got close to him in these last weeks; I almost always thought of him now in terms of his ridiculous first name—had gone off frightened, too. Frustrated, but most of all frightened at his own intrepidity. He was a scared blackmailer. Was that not likely to make him dangerous? Plainly, and I wondered why, he had come to hate me as I hated him. How much gin had he needed to get up his courage to go even this far? How much would he need to steady his weak nerves and his wobbling knees after seeing me? A good deal, I rather thought. Quite enough to make him thoroughly drunk, dozy, and incapable.

It was at that moment that the desire gripped me. I can only describe it as a thirst. Once it enters the mind, it penetrates the whole physical organism. The throat, the mouth, the stomach, even the head, the hands.

Have you ever wished to kill a man, Van der Valk? You are a policeman and it is conceivable, even quite likely, that you have pointed a firearm at some shadowy and fugitive figure. When you pressed the trigger, did you wish to kill? Did you feel that thirst? I am told that the pressing of the trigger can in certain conditions produce instant orgasm. I am not concerned with that. I can only recall a thirst so insistent . . . I wished to kill. Have you? Have you?

My mind now worked with startling ease and rapidity. If I were to react to Cabestan very quickly and suddenly indeed . . . The blackmail I had already forgotten. It was a small mechanism in my mind, I think

153

—what one might call a percussion cap. The explosive charge was my hate.

If I put Casimir off with words, and even if I paid him a large sum that I could later take steps to recover, he would suspect that I was planning malice. Once in fear of his miserable existence, he would try to do something to insure it. Hardly the Medical Association—not as long as he thought there was the faintest chance of money. But perhaps some third person. I did not know who it might be, just as I did not know what exactly he had heard. But he would certainly be in high hopes over the next twenty-four hours that I would climb down. Little he knew me, nor of what ferocity and finality I was capable. I was going, I saw, to react to M. Cabestan with a suddenness that would surprise both of us.

Two hours after he had left, I decided that he was sufficiently far gone in his cups. Ring the doorbell indeed! M. Cabestan appeared to have forgotten, so little interest had I always shown in his doings and movements, that I possessed the keys to his doors. I had been sitting without lights a long while, accustoming my eyes to dark. Finishing my cognac, enjoying a cigar. Yes, by that time enjoying. I had collected, still in the dark, a hypodermic syringe, a pair of surgical gloves, a bottle containing gin, as much money as I could lay my hands on, and two or three trivial household objects. Half an hour later, Casimir, who had been foolish enough to get extremely drunk, breathed his last in a coma. He had noticed nothing from beginning to end; I doubt that he even felt the hypodermic needle. I spent some time then, determined to be clearheaded, seeing whether anything could have been left—by him, not by me—that could point my way when he was discovered. I found nothing, and reflected that I would have a better opportunity within a day or two.

I went home. Beatrix had returned and gone to bed, unconscious that I had been walking softly about just over her head. I tidied, went to the kitchen, and had a glass of hot milk. I reviewed matters in bed, but I fell very rapidly asleep. Even the pain of thinking about Suzanne had been effaced—or, more accurately, excised under anesthesia.

You are going to say that I am a doctor. Had I no professional conscience? As a doctor, was I not aware of the value—the sacredness, as we are emotionally told—of life? I think that it was not the doctor who killed Casimir. I do not think it was even the man. I think that Casimir was killed by the young student who loved Suzanne, who was a bare three years older than she was. An adolescent. In adolescence, one feels nothing of this weightiness of life. That is why adolescents make the only satisfactory soldiers. The adult who makes a really good soldier has a narrow, rigid, and, I am certain, unbalanced mind. He has many of the characteristics of the psychopath.

9

The day following the next, I was drinking a cup of cocoa at around ten-thirty in the morning—a bright, warm, sunny summer morning—and resting for five minutes between patients, when Miss Maas came in. I looked up a second in some surprise, for she never disturbs me at work unless she has very good cause. I thought a patient had probably canceled. Recall that I was occupied with my work, which I am good at. Casimir was simply not in my mind.

"Forgive me, but I thought I should ask you. I have a slightly agitated young man outside, with some involved tale about the lodger."

Miss Maas has several small harmless snobberies and has always referred to Casimir in this way, generally once a year when the accountant comes to go over my income and arrives at checking taxes, rates, and so on, calculated for the third floor.

"I think we may have to intervene. The lodger, it seems, does not answer his bell, and hadn't yesterday either, and this young man fears a mishap. It occurred to me that we have keys; they'll be in the safe. Should I perhaps go myself, or should I look for a patrolling policeman? Mrs. van der Hulst is in the upper waiting room whenever you're ready for her."

"I think that sounds sensible, Miss Maas."

The conclusion was reached when I emerged at lunchtime. Miss Maas had immured the police—a plainclothesman by this time—in the lower waiting room, where I noticed that the daily girl had been a bit negligent with her dusting that morning.

"Very sorry indeed to trouble you, sir. I think we have all the available facts from your secretary; she's been most helpful. It's simply that since you are the owner of the property, sir, I thought it best to explain to you. . . ."

"I'm afraid I've been busy with patients the whole morning and haven't yet the least idea. Can you just give me a brief account?"

"Sorry, sir, of course. Gentleman upstairs is dead,

156

I'm afraid. Wasn't in good health, as we hear, and been drinking heavily—habitually, too. He must have collapsed up there and not been able to call for help; there's no phone there, either, and it's high up, of course. We've had the police doctor—heart failure, night before last probably, and we've taken him away. There's just his property and things, and that's on your premises, sir. Oh, here's your keys again. I forgot to give them to the lady."

"I'm sorry to hear all this. I hardly knew him at all, but he's been a fixture here in the house since before my time. What about family, and so on?"

"Can't tell yet, sir. Young man who came is an acquaintance, but knows nothing, he says. I thought you might have known, perhaps."

"I'm afraid I have no idea, but I feel a certain responsibility. Maybe the bank would know?"

"That's a thought."

"Perhaps if the bank feels able to send someone around, he could come and see me, and I will help in any way I can."

"Very obliging of you, sir."

I took the keys, sent Miss Maas for lunch with the remark that I would have to go and see about this, and went up those stairs, noticing calmly now a step that had alarmed me two nights before by creaking. I was simply being forced to play the polite hypocrite for a day, a thing I had had to bear in mind throughout. The police had rummaged about hurriedly looked for a clue with which to shuffle off the bother, and had not found the tape recorder, any more than I had. When I came upon it, I noticed there was a very long cord to the microphone, which, I calculated, when it was dangled out of the window, would be just right to reach my veranda windows. It seemed an amateurish and inefficient way of spying. Still . . . I satisfied myself that Casimir had left nothing else; his hiding places for things were obvious.

The bank, since this was an unrewarding affair, sent a minion, a foolish young man who groveled before me in the stiff phrases that had been taught him. We went through all papers. I felt confident that I could handle anything that might crop up, but there was nothing. We unearthed some cousin in the provinces who could be called on to arrange the funeral and get rid of the belongings. . . . It was all very simple, and a phone call to the manager of the bank the next day convinced me that there was nothing amiss. I instructed Miss Maas to send flowers, which I am sure she did with her usual skill and taste.

10

You have grasped, my dear Van der Valk, that in a sense I killed Casimir in order to inherit his flat—I could almost say his life. That flat magnetized me.

I had, naturally, a pretext. It was a little problem. I could not allow it to remain empty, nor did I want another tenant, and I never even considered reconverting the house to its four original stories. I do not think you were altogether surprised to find that I had practically moved up to the flat, though I pretended to you that I spent only a little time there. I needed to make no changes. The cousin from the provinces had decided that the cheap furniture was not worth the trouble of moving out, and suggested himself simply leaving it there for a new tenant. The good man!

There was nothing on the spools of the tape recorder; that is to say, there were scraps of conversation, since evidently I have my windows open sometimes, but it was an inaudible gabble. The tones of my voice could be distinguished, and there were other plainly feminine tones, some of them recognizable—to me—as those of Bella, but there was no criminal conversation. I did not know how often or for how long Casimir had tried this trick, but, however pertinacious, he had not been successful. Nothing had been achieved that way.

Just what way had it been achieved?

Bella is a delightful woman. She is a little too noisy, but she is warmhearted, charming, and amusing. She is not conspicuous for brains, her education is sketchy, and her contrast with Beatrix is complete. She has sense and character, and, being a good mimic, she has fitted herself excellently into her local milieu, that of big business. Her husband is the director of a merchant-banking firm, with large financial interests. A man of sixty, somewhat desiccated but not uninteresting. I know little about him, but enough; I treated him once. He does not ask much of her but to provide the usual comforts and amenities, like entertaining, which she does well, I imagine. She knows how to charm, how to talk the hostess jargon, and I am sure that her food and drink and flowers are admirably organized.

She came to me with the usual nervous troubles of a pretty, energetic woman of forty who has not enough to do. Absolutely banal complaints like chronic constipation, common to all these women. She has a fashionable house doctor, who often sends me patients; he is very conscientious and very busy, and since they have plenty of money, he sends them to me. I always send them back cured.

She is one of the women whom I have come to feel real affection for. Certainly Bella has given me plenty of affection back, though at the start she was simply a woman to my taste. I recall how pleased I was when I first saw her: her enchanting warm smile, her enthusiastic voice, her pleasure in simple little things, her naïve snobbery—a nice person. She had all the attributes I find attractive; she is like a very good cake. Everything about her is right—her furs, her perfume, her lacy silky wealthy underclothes. Her figure was and is admirable, and she had just the right mixture of provincial beliefs and little petty moral rigidities. I enjoyed her immensely even before I came to value her.

I telephoned Bella, and she came to see me for a "checkup." She was in good health and looked splendid. She gave my cheek an affectionate little tick with her rings.

"Naughty," she said, going off to the bathroom.

"How is Suzanne?" I asked when she returned putting her weapons back into her handbag.

"She's all right. Tiresome, yes, but I'm hoping now she'll grow out of it. There's so much that is new at that age; one forgets quickly."

"Never any disagreeable aftertaste from our arrangements?"

"Not the slightest."

That, anyway, put me at ease. Casimir had either not dared or not known enough for certain to approach

160

Bella with requests to keep him comfortable in his old age.

There I was, in perfect security. Till you walked in.

We have come to your third visit. In the course of the first two, I had had an uneasy suspicion that you might one day come to detect me. But it was on this occasion that I felt, for the first time, the certainty that you had understood. Not only that you were capable of understanding.

You asked abruptly to see Casimir's flat. I had told you off about poking in my house, but I had no way of objecting to this request.

"You will have keys, no doubt?" Of course you knew this; it was in the police report, I am sure.

"Oh, yes; they're even in my pocket." You would see anyway that I had them in my pocket. "I've been rearranging the flat. There was some old junk that needed clearing out."

We walked up the stairs.

"I spend some time up here myself." I let it fall coolly; I wasn't going to let you think you had me at a disadvantage.

"A refuge?" you said, cocking that nasty pale-blue eye of yours.

"Perhaps a game. I had never set foot here, you know; I was agreeably surprised to find out how pleasant it was. I have decided not to consider a new tenant. The one drawback is that interminable staircase."

"It should be a spiral staircase. Then you would be in a lighthouse—seductive feeling." You seemed to be talking to yourself.

"And who keeps it clean?" you asked. "You do that, too." People's household arrangements, even trivial

161

details, have a lot of importance to you; I have noticed that. You roamed about, stared out of the window, leaned out and peered at the garden below. My back room stuck out just there where the veranda used to be, and I wondered whether you had thought of Casimir's idiotic tape-machine trick.

You sat down on the divan, a narrow cheap thing from some chain store. I sleep on it three or four times a week. I had not accepted Casimir's bed, a scrap too personal an object. My own bedroom is a great deal more comfortable, but there is only a door between Beatrix and myself. I sleep very well up here.

You were sitting on the divan now, turning over some of my bedside books. You glanced up with—it sounds odd, I know—something like respect. I do not think I can be altogether wrong. I was studying you, too, for I had the sudden knowledge of a bond between us. This was increased when I noticed with amusement that you no longer looked like a policeman, for you had the look of simple pleasure that anyone who likes books gets with a book between his hands. At that moment, you had, I can swear, no interest in crime or criminals. You were feeling, too, I knew, for contact between us. I thought then that you would not try to arrest me, however much evidence you possessed, before making a genuine effort to grasp for understanding of the things you did not know, would never know.

Is it not to help you in that, and that alone, that I have written a thick loose-leaf notebook?

It is not a need of being understood. I have made that clear already. It is more the friendship that exists between soldiers who fight against each other. I have no friends of this sort, perhaps because I have never been a soldier; my military service was first deferred and then canceled. Perhaps because I have never given the kind of gift one needs for friendship. To have suffered together? I am groping; it is one of the closed books to me.

You were turning over a book now that I picked up recently out of a casual coincidence, for the writer has the same name as myself. A South African Dutchman —become English since, but without losing the grip on his own country—a Colonel van der Post. The book has a banal, probably deliberately understated title. The name is all we share, and it is a common enough Dutch name. I have never served in the army, let alone become English, I have never been in Africa bar a holiday once—should I use the word "honeymoon"?—in Tunis; I have never been in a Japanese prison camp; I have never climbed a mountain; I have never forged friendship. There lies, perhaps, my fascination with this book.

You were searching for some memory, turning pages.

"There is, somewhere, a letter to his wife. No, from his wife—I have it."

Your voice loses its professional monotony when you have a book in your hands, reading from it.

It seems to me that people's private and personal lives have never mattered as they do now. For me the whole of the future depends on the way people live their personal rather than their collective lives. It is a matter of extreme urgency. When we have all

163

lived out our private and personal problems we can
consider the next, the collective step.

You looked at me with no grin for a minute; then
the harsh lines reappeared with the two huge furrows
alongside your mouth. I thought you looked tired and
battered and middle-aged, though you are several
years younger than I am.

"Thought for today," you said hatefully. And went
back down to the consulting room. And picked your
everyday policeman's hat off the peg, with your everyday policeman's look back on. And the grin well in
place.

"Au revoir, Doctor. You're a very patient patient."

11

I do not think that the trouble lies anywhere but at
Beatrix's door. She quite certainly knows that I seduce women patients, though she has never alluded to
any such thing. But she is a most accomplished spy.
She would be quite capable, I am sure, of setting afoot
this mysterious oblique approach to me that culmi-
nates in your visits.

But I hardly think she can be your witness. Coming
as she does from a legal and judicial family, she
knows all the roundabout ways of the law, can get advice secretly, and could certainly keep out of trouble.
Added to this, she would never entangle her famous
family by being behind a legal attempt to put an end
to me. Too likely to compromise those gentlemen. She
is alive to every sort of ecclesiastical nicety; she would
have done no such thing.

No, I have thought carefully. Can it be Suzanne? In that case I am a dead goose, trussed and stuffed for roasting. For Suzanne, you see, has been my only real crime. I have sometimes wondered whether Beatrix, who might well know about Bella, may not have so arranged things that Suzanne should meet Casimir. It is farfetched, perhaps. Suzanne is, after all, an art student; she might have met him anywhere. He would be regarded, of course (she told me so herself), as old-fashioned and even meretricious by the rising generation. She tried to conceal from me that she knew him; I found it out only by accident.

There has been no crime but for Suzanne, or you could say perhaps that there would have been no crime but for Suzanne. For everyone will be pretending that my life is extremely reprehensible, but that, as you know and I know, is claptrap. All very dreadful, no doubt, and I would be expelled from the Medical Association with some very high-flown sorrowing phrases. But I have never done any of these women the slightest harm. If I say it myself, I have done most of them a lot of good. A definite therapeutic effect. I may have scratched some moralities, but criminal—never. Let us, besides, please not be hypocritical. Give the private life of twenty other doctors the attention you are giving mine, and you will receive a surprise. The capacity that women have for falling in love with their doctors—remarkable, my dear Inspector. I dare say, even, that it has happened to you.

Nevertheless I am ashamed of myself.

There is, of course, criminal conversation with children under the legal age of consent—I do not know the legal terminology. That, I quite agree, is vicious.

Still, Suzanne was a ripe sixteen and well developed for her age. Mentally, Van der Valk, mentally, in case you find an inclination to smile at these words.

Bella came to me one day, a few months ago, in a great state. "I want to ask your help. I have complete confidence in you, and indeed you are the only friend who can help me." Friend! There is considerable affection between Bella and myself, as well as shared secrets, jokes, and a large amount of pleasure. Does she think of that as friendship?

I lit her cigarette for her. As always, she was looking luscious.

"But any little thing I can do . . ."

"It's for my daughter—for Suzanne." I raised my eyebrows. "She's only sixteen. She's pregnant. I want to ask you—indeed, I beg of you." I must have assumed an unsympathetic expression. "Will you do something? Must I put it in crude words?"

"You are asking a difficult thing, you know, my dear. It is not one of the things I do." You may be surprised, but this is true. I have been approached often with the same request—what doctor hasn't—and have always turned it down flatly. First, it is criminal —yes, I distinguish, and without hypocrisy.

Second, it is tricky. I can do it safely, of course, without risk; that is not what I mean. I mean that there is chatter. It is inevitable that such practices become widely known.

Last, I have an objection. Even a moral objection. Oh, not exactly the conventional moral objection, the one advanced by moralizers who have never been in touch with reality. More a personal feeling that I am barred from doing such things. Beatrix, you see, is

sterile. Let me be utterly honest. She has always refused to get a medical opinion, which she says is humiliating to her. Humiliating! Bitch, useless bitch,
caring that a doctor should know that she admitted
suspecting herself. But I have never known for certain
about myself. The women I make love with take extreme pains. Once or twice, I have been asked to
make a woman pregnant. And I have not succeeded.
Nowhere do I know of a child that belongs to me. One
time, long ago, a girl delighted me by becoming pregnant, though she herself had no importance, but I
found later that the child she bore could have had any
of half a dozen fathers. I had to find out, you see.

I cannot be certain I am not myself sterile. That
has given me an overpowering reason for my refusal
to take children away from other people. If I cannot
create, I may not destroy. Does that make any sense
to you?

Bella, however, had more to say. "I can see that
you're thinking I am just like all the others that you so
despise. You are scared of what the neighbors would
say. You will tell me to send her abroad or even to
get her married. It's not that, though. I'm really concerned for Carl."

Carl is her husband. I have never told her so, but I
know him, for I have treated him. I even like him. He
came to me a year or so ago, with hypertension. I
need not go into that. I helped him. I found him sympathetic, and for a reason I have just given: he wished
for children of his own. He is a rigid person, naturally.
He would not run after women. Bella did not want to
have another child. He had said nothing, but he had
transferred the devotion he had for his wife to Su-

167

zanne. He was immensely proud of her, wrapped up in her.

Enfin, the usual tale: the child kicked against this concentration of affection. From her mother she had a less intense, more casual attention, and the mother got confidences in return that the unhappy fellow did not get. The girl had fallen among art students, and taken courses at the Conservatory, or whatever they call it. If Carl, a Christian businessman if ever I saw one, found out about this unlucky pregnancy, he might turn and rend the girl. Bella was, of course, even more concerned at the idea that he might turn and rend Bella.

When, after a long minute's silence, during which she had the sense to hold her tongue, I accepted, or showed signs that I might accept, I did not indicate that I was thinking as much of the man as of the woman, or the girl.

"I have to know more. Does the girl herself want this child?"

"She doesn't know—at sixteen, how can she know? She isn't at all happy at the idea of a bond with the father. I've checked—an unpleasant, rather undesirable person all around. Took advantage of her in a mean-minded way—got her drunk, the little idiot, after the warnings I've given her." I made up my mind with difficulty. Had I some notion that the step meant my undoing?

"If," I said slowly, picking my words, "you were to find a pretext for my seeing her that she would accept, I might find means to terminate this pregnancy without her being aware of the fact. How far is she?"

"Two and a half months."

"Not too bad. How's her general health?"

"Good. She's perhaps a scrap on the anemic side."

"That might serve. A miscarriage at three months is not unusual. I must warn you that one such sometimes seems to involve a tendency toward more."

"Oh, my dear, I would be grateful all my life. I simply daren't risk Carl's finding out." In her relief she was letting slip what really worried her. "Carl would quite assuredly throw all the blame on me, and in shock, rage, horror—believe me, you don't know my husband—he might do anything."

It was ironic that she did not suspect that this famous husband was exactly the reason I agreed. I disregarded the outburst tactfully.

"Send her to me."

12

They were fateful words. A week later, Suzanne was sitting in the chair opposite and I was playing the heavy. "Well, young lady . . ." Pompous puffwit that I was.

I may have been pompous, even a little adrift, right from the start, because I am not accustomed to young girls. I see few, and have never been altogether at my ease with them. I can explain that, and will, perhaps, in the course of this narrative. What I cannot explain, Van der Valk, is first that I found her desperately desirable, and second that I fell—yes, "fell," it is the only word—in love with her. With a girl of sixteen. To explain . . . A phrase comes into my mind from some book or other. Disraeli said, to an English duke on some occasion, "My dear Henry, never explain." There is no wiser counsel. But I cannot explain, even had I wished, and I do wish, I suspect. I have come to wish to explain everything to you.

She was slightly anemic; it was not serious. I went into a patter; she had had colds. She said without hesitating, quite simply, that she was pregnant.

"Yes." I was giving her a general examination; she had undressed unself-consciously and was lying on the couch. "I see as much. Well, that makes it all the more important to get you in good shape. I would have suggested a good holiday in the sun, but soon you won't be wishing to wear a bathing dress. Never mind. We'll give you some artificial sunlight." For I intended to give her some harmless ultraviolets and slip in a much shorter wave, in which I am proficient—a type of deep X ray that I knew would "do the trick," as it is revoltingly called.

I cannot explain either my tension or her abrupt encouragement of my vicious instinct. She has a splendid body, unusually finely formed for a girl of that age. Bella's body, and Bella's internal noises, I noticed while listening to her. But I had myself under control —I am a doctor, after all. My voice was calm, as always, my eyes masked from her candid blue look.

Had she some suspicion of the relationship between myself and her mother? Bella had perhaps been a little indiscreet in getting her to come and see me. Had she wished to get me in some way in her power? Had she some youthfully cynical contempt for men in general, acquired from her recent experiences? I have no idea. I cannot tell. You worry about it, if you will.

For she deliberately encouraged me, and I lost my head.

I can only relate that for a month she came for

treatment. And I was possessed by passion for that girl. I made a beast of myself the way one does sometimes in a very expensive restaurant. And I loved her. In a way I have loved no one.

A month. Then she simply stopped coming. Bella came one day afterward and told me that Suzanne had had a harmless, painless miscarriage. She was much relieved. She kept saying so. She said that Carl knew nothing, that the family doctor knew nothing, that she had fixed everything, and that she was eternally grateful. To show how grateful she was, she pelted into the back room and took her clothes off in a real hurry. I am fond of Bella. I tried to oblige her out of politeness.

I suppose you have understood. I found out quite by accident that Suzanne was acquainted with Casimir. I saw her once, after she left me, go toward his door. I imagined that Casimir—idiot that I was, for what grounds could I conceivably have?—was the "unpleasant, undesirable person" of Bella's fears. That Casimir, and no other, was the father of the child that I was busy getting rid of. The child I would have so greatly desired, and so greatly desired from that young girl of sixteen . . .

Once more, irony has overtaken me. For when I asked Bella to come and see me the last time, in order to satisfy myself that no effort had been made at blackmailing her, I asked, in a casual turn of phrase, whether she had seen anything of Suzanne's troublemaker.

"Oh, that, no no, thank heaven," she said quite airily. "A young man called Simons, whom I've never seen, but from all I've ever heard I felt quite sure he

171

was objectionable. Suzanne's quite got over that, at least."

Suzanne? I have never seen Suzanne since. I think she regarded me as a catharsis for the whole episode. Looking back now, I feel sure that she knew all along that I was employing means to abort her. And even that her mother had sent her to me for that express purpose. I would not be in the least surprised to learn that the very thought of me now made her sick.

I think, Inspector, that this episode comes under the heading of criminal conversation. Don't you? I am not proud of it.

And poor old Casimir. I should have told him simply to go to hell. With his tape recorder and his cheap binoculars and his eavesdropping. And every word he uttered giving him away for the mangy old dog he had become. Nobody would have listened to him for a second. I had not the slightest need to stamp on him in that frenzied way. Obliterating a poor harmless old sot whose simple pleasure was gazing at the windows opposite, where typists changing their dresses after work can sometimes be espied in their underclothes. He was not as much of a criminal as I was.

A thought has just struck me. I think now that Casimir hated me, and for the identical reason that I hated him. I think that while he was spying he had seen Suzanne leave my house. Knowing what he already did, I think he jumped to the conclusion that I had seduced her. I think that he may have loved her, in much the same ridiculous, absurd way that I did—and do—myself.

In killing Casimir, did I kill myself?

13

I am sitting up in the top-floor flat, quite alone, in Casimir's studio. It looks almost as if the summer had died suddenly, violently, for it is cold and rain is beating fiercely on the windows. I understand that the little gas fire would not have heated the studio enough in winter. Also it makes an annoying hissing sound, and I have preferred to light Casimir's oilstove. I have had to shut the windows, and the paraffin makes the room stuffy and smelly. I am changing: a month ago it would have been impossible for my fastidious nose to remain five minutes in a room with the thing. Now I am almost enjoying it. I have always had a sensitive nose, even as a child. . . .

Now, I had resolved to have none of that. I had determined to avoid the imagined-psychoanalytic nonsense whereby scarring episodes of childhood and youth are presented with a flourish in novels. The author, the fool, claps himself upon the back in self-congratulation and says "How clever am I" as he presents some worthless fiction as a justification for the unreality, the pretentiousness, the imbecilities that the worthless poltroon uneasily knows have filled his print-wasting pages.

There is truth in it though, alas. There are episodes in one's childhood that one always remembers. And they can be so trivial. Why should one remember them if it were not that one knows they left a permanent mark? Ah, "knows"—what does one ever really know? Still, I am as detached as any man. And since I said in my last installment that there were things I now wished to show you to allow you to draw your own conclusions—I do not pretend or wish to "explain" anything at all—so be it then.

I doubt, in fact, whether anyone can really pinpoint with accuracy hours or days that later gave direction to his character. I fancy, though, that anybody with training can give some indications. Take this rain, now. It is a summer's day, although the fine weather has been broken off like a branch struck by summer lightning. Heavy rain is falling out of an overcast sky, with a fairly strong westerly wind and a temperature in the fifties. On a day just before such a one—there may have been sun or there may have been cloud, I do not recall—I, aged seven, went to school in the neat, tree-lined, clean streets of the provincial town of my childhood. There were no buses then with automatic doors, but primitive-looking streetcars with open platforms. It was our pride, as children, to finish the ride on the bottom step and hop off some distance before the car ground to a stop. The bigger children gauged with absolute precision the speed at which they could jump as against the chance of having an ear grabbed by the grimy-fingered elderly conductor and being held until the streetcar stopped altogether—a disgrace, though it could happen to anybody. Rather like the paratrooper Colonel Langlais, who broke an ankle in the first jump over Dienbienphu! Indeed, the bigger children had for us, the seven-year-olds, all the glamour of paratroopers.

I had never dared jump, myself, and had perforce cravenly to wait with a group of other timid ones till the old streetcar had lurched to its standstill. One morning—this morning—I jumped, and at a speed that only lordly eleven-year-olds could attempt. I was determined, you see, to "get my wings."

I had, however, never grasped the trick of the three or four rapid pattering steps in the wake of the momentum. I leaped out at right angles, stumbled erratically, gyrating, through bewildering space, tripped over the gutter, and tumbled on the pavement, my head coming hard against a tin trash can, and fortunately not the ornate cast-iron lamppost to which it was wedded. Several sympathetic middle-aged women picked me up and took me into the nearest shop, where a kindly butcher deposited me on a slab and poured cold water on me. I came to and was violently sick.

"Oh, the poor lamb," said the women, a thing they would never have said to the other lamb, hanging above me on a hook.

"He'll be all right," said the butcher soothingly. "Where do you live, sonny?"

I suppose I told. The butcher, possessor of a Citroën delivery van (yes, it was a Citroën; I recall it perfectly), deposited me on some more or less clean sacks smelling only slightly of blood—so that it may have been the smell of sacking that promptly made me sick again—and took me home, where my dear mother grew rather alarmed. The butcher calmed her down, and she recalled that she had recently followed a grandiose First Aid to the Wounded course. (Evening classes were organized in the singularly gloomy urine-scented building of the lyceum, even more petrifying after twilight, but adults, I had remarked, were indifferent to such things.) She diagnosed concussion, quite sensibly, wound me in wet compresses, gave internal treatment of linden tea and aspirin, and put me into bed.

Our house at the time was a large ostentatious villa —I was ten or so before we got "poor." It had turrets and gables, stood in a quiet heavy street where all the shopping was brought by errand boys, and had a garden with evergreen oaks and a copper beech. It was called, of course, The Beeches. Firmly, in the plural, according to the current snobbery that a suburban villa was a townsman's country mansion. (The house next door was called Normandy and on the other side was Montreux, and both had tennis courts.) I had—being the youngest, the only son, and a great treasure—a room of my own, the "tower," which had two lancet windows and an octagonal shape.

Next day—the day it rained—I was kept in bed. I had a very slight headache and was otherwise in rude health. After my dear mother had fussed about with bread and milk and tiptoed out, I sat up. I wolfed the two dry rusks that had been left me, abolished the beastly cold compresses, and reached for a book. I spent there, with the rain hammering upon the tiles and windows of the turret—my crow's nest—the happiest day of my life. Quite alone, in a warm ecstatic nest, thinking occasionally, between more highly colored fantasies, of all the other little boys, suffering in their smelly inky classroom with the opaque globular lampshades that spread an acrid stink of heated dust. I hated and dreaded school.

I was a fidgety child, frail and timid. I was quick at reading and spelling, and always had the "recitation" and the verses by heart while the class was still struggling with the first line and a half up to the semicolon. But figures were a nightmare to me. To this day, I am confounded by nine sevens and seven eights. The decimal point was to me a maniac dot, invented by scholarly sadists. It flitted about among the rows of noughts, utterly uncomprehended, and poisoned my life. The classical "passage from one ten to another" pushed me with contempt and derision to the bottom of the school, and I suffered. What would have been my lot had I had to wrestle, like an English child, with pounds, shillings, and pence?

Every day we had a "maxim." This was a pious thought written the first thing every morning by the master, in superb flowing longhand at the very top of the blackboard, and it stayed there till the following morning, when it was erased with hieratic gestures by a long hairy hand, projecting from a grubby flannel cuff and the shiny sleeve of a soutane, holding a thing that looked like a clothesbrush but that had a sort of pad instead of bristles. I can still see it, sewn in a blue-and-white jelly roll of some woolly dishcloth material.

When we did our homework, we had to write at the top of the page, very neatly, name and Christian name, date, the Jesuit motto "A.M.D.G.," and this maxim, which we were trained to copy into our notebooks the moment it appeared. I fought, even then, an instinctive war against all maxims, and did this with the greatest distaste. My writing was uncontrolled and sprawling, and I always lost marks for imperfect transcription of those ornate flourishes signaling a capital letter's dreaded approach.

Horror—one winter evening I found that I had forgotten the maxim, and without it my homework would receive an inexorable zero. It was that kind of educational system; work counted for nothing if the seven-year-old was not thoroughly impregnated with some literary nun's idea of Bernadette Soubirous's good solid sense.

My mother was adamant. Back I had to go, under dripping-wet ghastly trees, through the black echoing "playground," past reeking dark sheds (lavatories, in the dark like the gas chambers of Auschwitz), into a building that was still open, because at the other end the big boys were still getting instruction hammered into their dirty ears. I crept into an empty classroom lit by an economical fifteen-watt bulb in the passage, and found that maxim, smug and imbecile on its blackboard, and ran home like a fury, in hysterical tears long before I reached The Beeches.

Next morning I got a zero after all. I had looked in Class 2.

14

It must have been a year later, and in Class 2, that I was so terrified at not knowing my tables one day that I never went to school at all. I left the house, naturally, at the given time, my satchel on my back. But I spent the whole day lying concealed in the belt of rhododendrons by the front gate, trembling as the baker's boy banged along the path whistling, a foot from my head, but unsuspected and undiscovered the whole blessed day. I was immensely proud of this achievement, and my confidence lent me a fluent mendacity when I said at school I had had to go to the dentist. I repeated the trick twice that year. I did not suffer from those hours lying in damp leaf mold. Indeed, no prison would appear to me brutal, no guard severe, even now.

From the age of seven, children who misbehaved were not punished with a tweak in the ear or even a backhander in class, but were sent formally with a note to the Prefect of Discipline, an aged tyrant who walked endlessly around the playground with his breviary. We in the top class of the preparatory department, aged eleven and bold with beginnings of muscle and pubic hair, maintained that inside the pages of the breviary he really had cowboy stories, folded small.

When a child reached this chalky old gentleman with one of the notes (there was no means of evasion, since after execution a second note was given, to be handed to the master originator of the court-martial), he would slip the cowboy stories into a side pocket of the soutane, read the note severely, and motion the criminal toward his office, a bleak little room ornamented with an extraordinarily elaborate roll-top desk. This walking to the office was the worst part of the punishment. For children as for adults, the leisureliness of justice carries the real sting.

Out of a back pocket, for those soutanes were ingeniously designed for the carriage of concealed weapons (and in the sleeves were stuffed large dirty clerical handkerchiefs), he then produced a Jesuit weapon, most painstakingly manufactured and well finished, officially called a ferula. It was a shiny thing of black stitched leather, something the shape of a narrow shoe sole, rather elegant, flexible, and springy. One then held out one's hand for Twice 2 or Twice 4, according to the gravity of the offense. Some recommended holding the hand limp and hollow, others keeping stiff and brave; the methods were equally painful. The maximum, in theory, was Twice 9, but there were dread tales of even worse beatings. I was beaten frequently, being dreamy, inattentive, fidgety, often disrespectful, and occasionally really wicked, as witness the time I discovered that by swallowing quantities of air I could presently send the whole class into hysterics by loud emissions of wind. I got Twice 6 for Disrespect, Creating Disturbance, Obscenity, and the grave crime known, I believe, to the army as Dumb Insolence. I was also beaten frequently for lying.

We measure time in decades: one is an infant till ten, a child till twenty, a youth till thirty. After that, one is just a man for thirty years, until one's sixtieth birthday and, I suspect, the beginnings of wisdom and decrepitude hand in hand. At the age of ten, I got from my father my first fountain pen, a rather superior one, black with a rolled-gold clip. Rolled gold sounds good but means, I believe, some cheap plating process. To a child, it is very fine.

I had surmounted the initial stage of the Jesuit school—Preparatory, Elements, and Figures. I was in Rudiments, and before me lay Grammar School, and the superior school, the names of whose classes I have forgotten, save two that were beautiful—Poetry and Philosophy. In Grammar School I met the one sympathetic action I was to encounter from the teaching staff throughout my whole school days—indeed, the one action approaching intelligence.

I consistently had the highest marks in the class,

save for one boy, a Jewish boy called David Gold. I have no idea why he was sent to a Catholic school, though he had bright-blond hair and a muscular Aryan exterior that would have pleased Heinrich Himmler. Certainly he made no effort to deny or conceal his Jewishness. He was good at gymnastics, for which I envied him bitterly; gymnastics were to me—those dread bars, those ropes, those harsh cocos mats, that smell of feet and carbolic—hell. I could box, though, much to my surprise, and Gold and I—the children called him Fish, of course—fought furiously. Once, he knocked half my left ear loose, and I still feel the tiny welt. He was, you will understand, my friend.

His parents were rich, and he turned up one day with a French dictionary, so new, shiny, and delectable that I was eaten up by the desire for it. I stole it, thinking that its newness made it untraceable. Alas the master, investigating, found Gold's name, written, after the fashion of children, very small, in pencil, at the extreme inside bottom corner of the back cover. I will always remember that master. He said nothing in public at all. He made me go quietly to Fish, admit my theft, and give back the dictionary. And he gave me another, as new and as shiny, that he had gone out to buy in the midday break.

I have said that this man was the one teacher with intelligence. That seems harsh, but I encountered in the superior classes nothing but a dull pedantry. There was nothing whatever to give a child the slightest pleasure in anything, outside the curriculum or in it. For a Jesuit school, it must have been a very bad one. I recall little of those years, save ludicrous episodes like the embarrassed cleric and Victor Hugo. I remained good at languages and bad at algebra. I got prizes at year end (of the genre Southey's *Life of Nelson*) and reprimands for not being able to trace the exact outline of Charlemagne's empire upon the map of Europe. I had frequent penitential excursions to the office of the Prefect of Discipline, and others to the Prefect of Studies, where the torment, though not corporal, was just as disagreeable and lasted much longer. I would be told that my parents paid reduced fees, and Made Sacrifices, and that Consequently. . . .

We were doing *"Booz endormi,"* an example favored by pedants for illustrating Hugo's less ranting manner, and had got to the line where Ruth is asleep with her breasts bare.

"Seins," said the pedant, mumbling, "means uh . . ."

"Breasts," said Gold, who had a sophisticated home life.

"Bosoms," suggested some other urchin.

"Tits," said a sotto voce at the back; some overgrown child with a huge dirty wink at various fifteen-year-olds who were corrupt in an innocent and fumbling way.

"Chest," said the pedant firmly, searching in his sleeve for a handkerchief. "Chest," defiantly. Fish kicked me under the desk; I sniggered, and was immediately sent to the Prefect for judgment.

I recall nothing of my lyceum years but trashy French verse. *"Oh combien de marins, combien de capitaines"* and the poetry for housemaids by Alfred de Musset. Was there no French prose? I suppose that there were approved authors, like Chateaubriand. Of

English literature, I recall the dreary set pieces by
Lamb and Hazlitt with titles like "A Cold Morning"
(somebody warming a razor in his bosom, surely an
extraordinary notion) or "On Going a Journey." English poetry seems in retrospect to have been suppressed along with the French prose, but it was that
kind of school. Those worthy and excellent clerics—
one is reminded of Stendhal's tutor, the Abbé de
Raillane.

15

It must mean something that Ruth's bosoms stuck so
fast to this capricious memory. I was certainly the
kind of child described by Raillane tutors as "pruri-
ent." I was precocious, nervous, easily touched by the
sensual. My mother, going through a Life Beautiful
phase just after the Kaiser's War, owned many elaborate books. It is the illustrations by Rackham and
Dulac, rather than the splendid *Don Quixotte,* by
Doré, that I recall. Hawthorne's *Wonder Book,* or
The Ring of the Nibelungen, with endless flexible
naked little girls; all these illustrators must have had
something of a Lewis Carroll complex. I recall one of
these books vividly, called *The Earthly Paradise,* or
some such name. It was bad verse, which I never read,
but each page was accompanied by a large arty pho-
tograph in the pearly halftones of the period. All were
of naked prepubescent girls on a beach, playing little
games with sand and reeds and shells, the mysterious
shadows between these children's slim elegant thighs
photographed with loving attention. Did these picto-

rial Annabels and Lolitas give me a taste for rounded women in their late thirties?

My memories of my father are vague. He was a big, robust man, who had made a lot of money as a mining engineer in Indonesia. There he had injured his health, maybe as a consequence of rheumatic fever. He also had a recurrent tropical malady that laid him up at intervals in a black depression. I think he may have been furious at his muscular body letting him down.

I was born in Indonesia, but within three years we were all brought back to Holland. My sisters, much older than myself, would talk about the wonderful life we had had there, but no colorful or uninhibited memory, no word of Malay, disturbs my placid Dutch childhood. My father had money placed in mines of various kinds, and we lived, as I have said, in a large hideous villa suitable to a well-off *rentier*. I recall glassed cases of geological specimens and others with daggers and shields, the bellicose handiwork of Dyaks or some such, which were less dull but with which I was not allowed to play. I recall the garden, damp and gloomy with overgrown laurel and rhododendron, and a house also damp and gloomy, with stained glass that lent mahogany and pampas grass a churchy feeling surely depressing to others as well as me, but nobody did anything about it.

My father's investments lost value steadily during the depression. My mother, who dramatized most things, was fond of saying that we were as poor as church mice, and that we should be on the street in our shirts at any moment. I cannot recall our suffering the slightest hardship. We never got to the bread-and-margarine-and-cocoa stage, like most people. But the house was sold, certainly at a huge loss, and we moved to a small poky house in a new, rather "working-class" district. I think my father suffered. He used to go out into the country, such as it was: splendid farming ground but flat and featureless. The drained land, and on one side the sand downs, were no substitute to him for the forest, the jungle.

I think that he was a nice person, because he made botanical drawings, a few of which I still possess. He would take a little sketch pad, and draw field flowers. At home he did these over, exactly, minutely, in India ink and water color, and wrote all the names he could discover underneath the drawings, in his printed engineer's script. The drawings are quite clumsy and naïve, but there is devotion in them. My mother was a nice person, too. You will notice the strange distance between me and my parents. Affection I had, and affection I returned, but there was always a gap of which I was aware.

She was a very pretty, gushing, talkative woman, from a family of important colonial administrators; an uncle of hers had been a Governor General. She had lost a good deal of caste in her family by becoming converted to Catholicism; she swam in emotional fervors with all a convert's uncritical joy. She had plenty of intelligence and much charm, marred by a certain tiresome silliness. She crowded the house with *bondieuserie*—pious pictures and holy-water stoups covered in sugar angels. She had a very showy missal, and a terrible rosary—of which she was very vain—of wood from the Mount of Olives, blessed it was said by a Pope. She poisoned my life with sentimental child

185

saints—wellborn of course, like Aloysius Gonzaga or Guy Fontgallant—and invited curates to the house for glasses of sherry.

Once we were poor, she maintained herself with innocent snobberies. She could not, of course, cook or do housekeeping, and that was not her fault, surrounded as her whole life had been with a flock of servants, but unwittingly she made me suffer. Hardship, I have said, there was none, but suffering there was. I was sent to the most expensive school. My sisters had been to expensive convents, but had finished, being much older, before the depression really made itself felt. They were now independent, with their own friends, and cared little. I was small and fragile, much mothered and babied, and had no such defenses. I was sent to school in the cheapest clothes. My companions played tennis, but we were too "poor" to afford a tennis racket. They had expensive bicycles; I had none.

They went for holidays, which we could not afford. Their clothes were elegant and their shoes of soft leather. I was sent to school in thick clumsy boots, and my mother was proud of the economies thus accomplished. Some of these things bit very deep. I have never forgiven that tennis racket. Or the shapeless cotton swimming shorts, which, when wet, hung on my shanks like paper, outlining my extremely self-conscious penis and causing snickers from children with solid wool shorts that had badges of swimming clubs stitched on them. Occasionally the kind mother of a rich friend—Mrs. Gold—would invite me for a free afternoon or even a day on weekends. My mother made me accept these invitations, quite rightly but inconsistently, and I see myself still climbing into the Golds' big luscious Talbot auto, wearing boots, clutching my cotton shorts, agonizing. Fish himself was much too nice a boy to comment, and Mrs. Gold and the chuckling cigar-smoking Papa Gold, who dealt in furs, showered me with kindnesses. But other children remarked with their natural cruelty upon my mother's petty snobberies and pettier economies.

My father did not notice such things. He had plenty of clothes himself, old but good for a lifetime. When on my twelfth birthday I begged and prayed for a bike, he gave me one, and saw that it was a good one. I think it is because of that bike and the rolled-gold fountain pen that I remember my father—quite unjustly, really—with more kindness than my mother. She could be extremely kind, but I wished sometimes that she would go to heaven with Guy Fontgallant—a little boy, as I recall, from an exceedingly wealthy and snobbish family—and leave me in peace.

I was not allowed to make friends with poorer children who wore boots; my mother said they had common accents and very likely ringworm, too.

With girls, of course, I had no contact whatever. Girls did not approach expensive Jesuit schools. I was eighteen and had won a scholarship to the University before I met and spoke with a girl of my age. That, Van der Valk, must seem extraordinary and unlikely to you, but I assure you that it is so.

In fact, I seem, on looking over these pages, to get a slightly bitter taste. That is fair, for I had, despite many solitary pleasures, an unnecessarily harassed and painful childhood.

There is a sense of needless stupidity in that combination of "standing" and cheeseparing, as there was in my father's dislike of bothering himself with sudden, perhaps shame-stricken, generosity. All that certainly widened the gap.

My father died in my first year at the University. He had quarreled, I believe, with his family, of whom I recall nothing but a portentous bearded brother and a faded sister at the funeral. I felt little emotion, perhaps a vague pity at his death. The gap had got too wide. I could spare only one day away from lectures and from Amsterdam.

My mother went to live with her sister, my Aunt Mathilde, in Voorburg, just outside The Hague; my aunt's husband, regarded as a high candidate for colonial honors, had died in Djakarta in administrative service while quite young. My mother really did this to get back to the atmosphere where she felt at home; the sisters drank tea with their friends and talked about the good old days, for Voorburg is populated with pensioned colonial widows as well as old gentlemen who have retired as full of honors as their houses are of tiger skins and Balinese dolls. But I was given to understand that this was done out of altruism, to save every penny and further my education. I was not impressed, or particularly grateful. I lived in a respectable lodging house—how well I remember it!—in Amsterdam, near the Museum, on the Jan Luykenstraat. I had henceforward money for books, a few clothes, and even some cheap amusements if I cared to discover any.

I had been sent to the University to study humanities—the Arts Faculty, as it is named pleasantly but vaguely. For my teachers had said that languages, living and dead, were my only real strength. True to principle, my mother had not the remotest idea of steering me toward some career that would earn me a living. Nor had I; so little notion of reality had I at eighteen that I planned to get a "good degree" and enter the Diplomatic Service.

Fish, still the only friend I had, despised "Arts," though he was even better at the disciplines than I was; throughout school I was eternally second to him. He was going to read medicine, and it was at his house, halfway through my first year, in the first flush of independence, that I was bitten by the bug. Theo Visser, then professor of materia medica, had come to dinner, and after a very good meal, Mrs. Gold's excellent coffee, Papa's wonderful Cuban cigars, and armagnac brandy, old Theo got so lyrical about medicine—the two boys sitting enraptured, their mouths slightly open—that I determined then and there to change over. Forgotten were the good degree in languages and the Diplomatic Service. I dawdled out the rest of the academic year reading all the medical books I could lay my hands on, went to no more lectures than were necessary in order not to get sacked altogether, and at the beginning of the next semester, to my mother's anguish, I plunged into "premedical."

That was the year of Munich. Papa Gold, no fool, was settled in Canada three months later, and Fish, my only anchorage, went with him. Mrs. Gold cried a little when I went to say goodbye. She was fond of me, and I think she understood me well enough. She gave me a check for three hundred dollars—three hundred dollars—from her own account, and Papa gave me a signet ring I still wear. Fish volunteered three years

189

later for the Canadian Army. He was killed in Holland, ironically, just at the time of the Liberation. I never saw him, though I was in Amsterdam throughout the whole war.

There you are, Van der Valk, my boy. You are, I think, in your late thirties—old enough to remember the years before Munich and the years of the depression, the years when things like schools were extraordinarily old-fashioned here in comparison with other countries, the last years of Holland's long isolation and comfortable dozy sleep that was to end only in the violent break-in of reality in the May days of 1940.

But we may as well go on, and even perhaps get all this threshed out in one sitting. Beatrix is expecting me for dinner, but I do not intend to go. Instead, I am proposing to do what I have never done before. I am going to eat at a cheap "lunchroom" restaurant, where there is music and a huge menu full of strange things, and people order the oddest combinations, like cold Russian egg salad with fried potatoes. The restaurants are open till late at night. I think I will enjoy this. I will take a pocket book with me—a Simenon, for instance—and read it at the table, and drink beer.

What on earth would anyone say who knew me, to see Dr. van der Post, who has certainly as high an income as any specialist in Holland, sitting in a lunchroom at ten at night, eating Russian eggs with chips, drinking beer and reading a Simenon, printed on lavatory paper, that rests on his plate's edge?

What would you say?

Would it please you to see me rub shoulders with the people of Amsterdam, those very "people" my mother found rather shocking? You are one of them yourself. You see, I am not so stupid after all.

My youth, yes. The twentieth birthday was a big landmark. I was halfway through "premed" and worried at not losing my virginity. In these days, no boy has any difficulty finding a girl of his own age to sleep with. In England, these girls wear little badges to proclaim their accessibility, and have contraceptives in their schoolbags. You recall, the yellow golliwogs? Rather a poetic conception. Or contraception, as you prefer.

But then. . . . Any town more provincial and puritanical than prewar Amsterdam is difficult to imagine. To find a girl to go to bed with—even at twenty, when I was smoking a big pipe and using ridiculous medical jargon—was a formidable undertaking.

Naturally, there was the old quarter. Nowadays it is a tourist attraction. Any young girl, even alone, can walk giggling through narrow alleys, peering with a greedy choky sensation at the girls behind the windows. And any boy with a few dollars in his pocket can push open the door and see the "girl" of his choice get up, bored, to draw the curtain, putting down her book or her knitting with a sigh, languidly undoing her skirt, fumbling at the zipper, with her free hand already held out for her money.

But before the war, you must know, the old quarter was a place of terror and legend. No well-brought-up person dreamed of going near it. Even policemen went there in couples. There were tales of drunken seamen robbed and knifed by a banditry that hid in the rabbit warren of attics and cellars. Legend went further. In the minute, stinking alleyways, there was cholera and

191

sleeping sickness, and in the attics (where, opening a tiny window, you might get a breath of tropical scents), there were even, it was whispered, lepers hidden. Amsterdam, you recall, was the great European port for the Far East, the visible, tangible, smellable link with Holland's empire, which was a tropical archipelago the size of the United States.

In fact, even as medical students, puffed with bravado, we shook in our shoes when we first came to the Binnen Gasthuis, the hospital that still stands on the demarcation line between the old quarter and the prim city, and has fingers, and toes, that are dabbled in the blood and pus of both.

There were women students, of course. Fewer than now, but quite a huddle in the Literature and History Faculties. They were mostly plain, with spots and stringy hair, and tended to come from earnest provincial families. They were stiff and proper, and lived boarded out with their uncles in the big city. Two, however, met my standards, which were exacting.

For I was a great admirer of beauty. A devotion to the senses, to the curving sweeping line, to nineteenth-century romanticism. Music, as yet, I knew nothing of. (My family was, in retrospect, strangely philistine. My mother, a great talker about books and pictures, never once took me to a concert or a gallery.) Books, however, there had always been in the house, and during my last lyceum years I had discovered Wilde and Beardsley, the Bakst and Benois designs for the Russian Ballet, the nudes of Titian and Giorgione, the verse of Théophile Gautier, and I was something of an adolescent aesthete. These two girls came within the definition of what was acceptable to such a person.

Marie was blond, with a little tilted nose, quiet, and neat, and rode on an expensive bicycle from her parents' superior residence near the Zoo. Her father was some departmental secretary in the municipal administration, a functionary of quite a grand sort. Marie was very much a little Sainte N'y Touche, her nose somewhat in the air. She was conscientious, went to all lectures, and took careful notes in a neat but stupid round backhand. I sat just behind her, did my best to smell her hair, and dared not say a word to her.

Alida I admired less; she was less well shaped. Taller, a little clumsier, with a suspicion of hair on her upper lip and her sturdy calves as well as her strong forearms. She had long brown hair with a reddish tinge, strong black eyebrows, long greenish eyes that gave vitality to her face, and a very pretty mouth. She may have been the only girl in the University to wear lipstick, then thought distinctly fast and decidedly common. She came, indeed, very nearly from the "people" and lived in a plain apartment at the very limit of Amsterdam-South, a district only just built.

I followed Marie home after I had dared, following a few abject failures, to speak some conventional greeting, to which she replied politely with a pleasant smile. And one weekend I dressed myself as killingly as I knew how to, polished my shoes and my hair, more or less with the same product, and knocked trembling at her door. She opened it herself, to my relief, looking surprised. I stuttered out some lame suggestion for the cinema; she looked even more surprised.

"Oh . . . Well I'd like to very much, but I'm afraid no, thank you, I can't." I must have looked stupefied as well as unhappy. "I'm afraid my father wouldn't let me. I'm afraid I have to go now."

She shut the door hastily, and I fled, dismayed. I never got the little mystery solved, since Marie continued to smile politely and say good morning, and once even asked for details of some lecture she had missed. Her fluster may have been due to the cinema, or to my being Catholic, for I was of good family, presentable, not too awkward (thanks to the Golds), not too grindingly poor, and not at all a wild student. However, both the cinema and the Catholicism might have made me untouchable to her sort of strait-laced bourgeois family, by no means uncommon then in North Holland.

I now saw Alida in a different light, and was not discouraged for long. Marie became a trifle insipid, while Alida seemed less earthy to my fastidious eye and the lines of her figure were athletic. . . .

I did not, after my rebuff, knock at any more doors, but I hung around Alida's district at night, saw her occasionally running errands, and discovered that her father was a head buyer in the big department store in the town, from which came her slightly loud winter coat and smart cheap shoes. The store had Catholic management, and some of the Protestants refused to buy there, despite the wide choice and low prices.

I did not pluck up the courage to speak to her till a lucky day when we asked simultaneously at the reading-room desk for the same book—Brunetière, I recall. I was as astonished to find myself a success with Alida as a senator from Mississippi would be to wake up and find himself President. She was simple and spontaneous. She never made me feel stupid or awkward; on the contrary, with her I felt an easy companionship. On sunny days we sat in the park, went rather hot and sticky to the cinema, and took long walks through the streets during the evenings of the last prewar summer. Our pleasures were very simple, and as simply I loved her.

To trace the course of all this in detail would be very boring. But in my youth as in my childhood there are salient moments that you will notice.

The pension on the Jan Luykenstraat, which was proper, and where no girl would have been allowed, was clearly impossible, and with "adult" daring I moved to another, scruffier, much gayer pension, on the Stadthouderskade, where the food was much worse but the company much better, where, indeed, I stayed throughout my student days. Everybody had his own pot of jam with a label stuck to it, and one frequently put one's feet through tears in the sheets.

I cannot forget dear Mrs. Koning, who lived all day in the basement with her fat musical daughter Naomi, who permanently wore an amazing hat with cloth parma violets on it, and who had a stain on her lip from the inseparable cigarette that was stuck in the corner of her talkative, friendly, vague mouth. I can recall, too, all my fellow lodgers: Mr. Veldkamp, the schoolmaster—he insisted on being called Mister—with dark curly hair, a thick mouth, and black-rimmed glasses, who was sensitive to drafts; Miss Obbema, a dry-looking woman with bifocals, fiftyish, who had "her" cushion, "her" chair, and a conviction that people stole her jam. Astonishingly, she was an artist.

Even more astonishing, an artist in stained glass and, I believe, a good one. Both she and Mr. Veldkamp were very orthodox and quoted the Bible frequently.

Quite the opposite religiously was Billy Kol, a medical student in his fourth year, old for his age and for his class. He was an atheist, a great fusspot, especially about his health, and anticlerical to annoy the "clerical party," whom he fought by stealing their jam, hiding their cushions, and sneakily opening windows behind the dusty plush curtains. He wore glasses, but was constantly leaving them off because of a lunatic theory that his eyes would get too dependent on them.

And the girls . . . Margie, who called herself Juana and was the mistress of—yes, Casimir, then possessor of a large reputation. She claimed, anyway, that she was his mistress, though she hardly left the house, where she stayed in bed all day reading and eating sweets. And Evelyn . . . But I am anticipating. The point of the move to the Stadthouderskade, a stone's throw from the Jan Luyken but mysteriously lower in standing, was to get Alida into the house. For we all had our own keys here, and came in at all hours, because of Mrs. Koning's aversion for ever leaving the basement.

With the first romantic tendernesses worn smooth, my boy's sensuality was stirred by Alida. To help me in getting her clothes off, a thing I was not exactly practiced in, I invoked the subject of Art. Her coltish body scarcely fitted the illustrations to "Salome" that were my ideal at the time, but I had at least understood that the female nude body is beautiful, made beautiful by an erotic element. After a good deal of argument along the lines of "How would any painter ever have managed . . . ," a shy, trembling, awkward

Alida stripped in the second-floor back room, left of the landing.

I had water colors, which I tried to use like oils, being in love with vivid color. I made bad pencil sketches with wandering lines and a most medical lack of anatomical knowledge, and colored them rather well, with splendid green shadows. Poor Alida! Perched in great discomfort on my bed, in the pose of Manet's "Olympia," a facial expression as though the worn rug under her were red hot! My eyes must have burned fiercely upon her juvenile figure; she fidgeted all the time, despite entreaties, and insisted on dressing after ten minutes, so bothered that she forgot to tell me to turn, and I sat biting my fingers.

Ah, I wore her down of course. When naked, she threatened to scream if I came near her, but there was a lot of moist breathing at other times, and I succeeded every now and then in getting past rather pathetic schoolgirl underclothes with tight elastic that would appear highly laughable to, let us say, Suzanne today.

My youthful virility never penetrated poor Alida's confused and tormented body. Once switched to another department of the University—and the Medical Faculty was in another part of the town—and hard at work, my interest in Alida ebbed. For I was good even at premedical, and was in the top two per cent of my classes throughout, however childish and confused I was by emotions. I imagined, being full of valuable premedical catch phrases, that she was "half-virgin" and therefore despicable, whereas the poor child would have made a good companion to anyone less gauche than myself.

It was not, of course, only Alida that disappointed

my longing for female flesh. My first efforts toward another goal were aimed at the ineffable Juana.

Margie was a figure of comedy in many ways. She had a plump, puppyish face and figure, long poker-straight pale-brown hair that flowed casually about her, and immense good nature. The hateful Obbema and the prig Veldkamp loathed her, and complained frequently of this slut to Mrs. Koning, who took no notice, let alone throwing her out as they demanded. She must have had hidden sympathy for the girl, who was indeed thoroughly nice, though stupid, and had no notion why anyone should dislike her. She spent hours in the bathroom, and would sail out smiling gently at the furious "next," bundled in an absurd peignoir and showing lots of exuberant bosom when she dropped her toothbrush, which she always did. Her room was a perfect sight, and one after another the maids gave up any effort to clean it; there was a sort of huge turnout about once a month. In between, it overflowed with dirty stockings—real silk, very grand for those days— showy but drafty underpants known to saleswomen as "French," bits of embroidery that never got finished, knitting for which the pattern had been lost, candy wrappers, and coffeecups with the dregs gone hard in the bottom. The walls were hung with large charcoal drawings, presumably the work of Casimir, of a very naked and fleshy Juana, which she could spend hours admiring. When the door was open—and it always was —one was hit, every time one passed, by these huge eyefuls. Juana washing her neck (good heavens, what sacrifices for art!), three-quarter back, Juana brushing her hair, one-quarter profile, Juana couchant, passant, rampant, and apparently needing to be naked whatever her activity. She was only slightly less naked in real life, and her favorite costume was a flappy pair of "beach-pajama" trousers, fashion of somewhere around 1937, with hibiscus blossoms on them, and a cardigan back to front, somewhat shrunken, outlining massive breasts with impudent menacing nipples, and precariously held by two buttons somewhere in the spine, generally in the wrong buttonholes.

However flaunted all this abundance might be, I got nowhere in my efforts to reach it. Margie went into shrieks and giggles when I got up my courage, drinking coffee in her room, to poke a finger at some plump curve, and hit me disagreeably on the knuckles with a hairbrush. But she remained generous with candy and paper-bound novels, and huge wafts of overscented face powder, till the war made all these goodies unobtainable.

The war brought a straitening of my circumstances —that money of my father's invested in Indonesia. Suddenly I had half the amount I was accustomed to live on. Mrs. Koning was unperturbed, and let me have one of the tiny attic rooms where the maids had formerly slept, very much under the eaves and with walls composed, as far as one could make out, of a few rough wooden posts connected by seventeen or eighteen layers of cheap wallpaper stuck together. There were no more maids, for the lumpish and reddened fruits of the backwoods now stayed there, sensibly; there was more to eat in the backwoods. Naomi still trotted to the Conservatory every morning with her violin in its case, and did the housework in the afternoons, helped by another girl, some classmate. Mrs. Koning slept in her treasure cave, where she kept rice

199

and bacon, oatmeal and brown sugar—and managed to keep it an amazingly long time. The rice got pretty wormy toward the end, but one did not notice the beasts, said Billy cheerfully, since they stopped moving about once they were cooked.

Next door to me, in the other attic room, lived Evelyn. She was a law student, two or three years older than I was, and had always seemed aloof and rather adult. We had never seen much of her, because she was poor and did not eat with us at the table, but had an alcohol lamp up in her aerie to which Mrs. Koning turned a kind of blank eye. She was thin and pale, anemic-looking, distinctly flat-breasted, with fearful salt-cellars at her collarbones. I would never have got to know this bony beauty—for she had good features and fine ash-blond hair—had it not been for the winter of 1941. Those attics . . . We heated bricks in the kitchen oven, put the next morning's washing water into stoneware gin bottles, and collected all the old clothes we could rake up. My mother sent me my father's old things, and I lived in a wonderful tweed Norfolk shooting jacket, and at night under a camel overcoat with many moth holes, but warm.

The night the oil froze in the German automatic weapons in Russia, Evelyn came into my room and asked awkwardly—she was blue with cold, and her pinched face looked transparent—whether we could not unite our resources. It was nothing but the need of animal warmth that drove us into bed together.

Of her two great fears, becoming tubercular and becoming pregnant, Evelyn took better precautions against the second. Never was I allowed to have her, though it was understood between us that I could touch her as much as I cared to.

In 1942, the despised Mr. Veldkamp was discovered to be a resister, and to have been extremely brave, which shamed us. He was, we heard later, arrested trying to get away to England and, I presume, shot. In 1943, Juana, who had got pastier and fatter, was taken to the hospital. A year later it was she, and not poor thin Evelyn, who died of tuberculosis. In 1944, the winter of hunger, there were fewer of us, and we were much better disposed toward each other, huddling together in Mrs. Koning's kitchen, the place in the house that stayed warm longest. Obbema was the last to go. Jamless but undefeated, still quoting the Bible at Billy (a real doctor now), penniless and upright, she survived the war. By the kind of irony that one grew accustomed to, she was hit by a military truck that skidded and mounted the pavement a few days after the Liberation. She died a few minutes later held up by Billy, her old enemy, while settling her bifocals back up between her ferocious eyes in a gesture familiar to us all.

Evelyn had gone before the hunger winter. She had family in Denmark, I think, and volunteered for some German work force hoping to get up into Schleswig-Holstein and cross the border there. We never heard from her.

It was in 1944 that I slept with a girl for the first time. She was blond, like Evelyn, thin, and washed-out, with adenoids and a fearful Amsterdam accent, a prostitute in the old quarter. She was surprisingly gentle with me. I went to her twice, but the third time she had pneumonia and I had to be content with the dark girl who shared the room. She was friendly, too, but smelled, and had such a professional manner that I had a fiasco. Kay had been professional but sensitive enough to see my predicament and be patient about it. She had smelled, to be sure, but with her I had at least accomplished what I longed for. Ludicrous, isn't it?

In 1946, my dear Van der Valk, I become a licensed medical practitioner, and had had just the amount of experience with the female body that I have taken such pains to describe for you. I went through every stage—collecting pornographic photographs, reading the very tedious and unimaginative literature on the subject, filling myself with fantasies about any girl I saw in the street whose skirt, perhaps, had stuck to her bicycle as she jumped off it, showing me a glimpse of thigh that would torment me for a week.

I am glad that my mother lived long enough to see me arrive at the threshold and the promise of a fine career. Life to her was such a simple affair that I am pleased that she had a quiet, simple death with no pain, convinced that now the war was over, the life she had always known, centered on Government House in Batavia, would resume the even tenor she had known, even if the ill-mannered boys and short-skirted girls of 1945 were not what she was accustomed to.

Old Theo Visser was long retired, but I called on him when we heard that my friend David Gold was dead. He used his influence among his friends and colleagues to get me a good job, and it was he who secured for me the postgraduate course in England, where I learned about neurological techniques that had been bought with the experiences of war. It was the first time I had ever been abroad, and I went off in high spirits, but the experience was unfortunate. I had always thought of England in terms of Rupert Brooke; I found instead the dismal uniformity that anyone who lived in England during the reign of Sir Stafford Cripps will recall. It was like Holland, with points and coupons and austerity, and a great many forms to fill in after one had queued for a considerable time. The subtle difference was, perhaps, dismaying, for the language of the English forms was not the abrupt—even rude —menace of dire happenings if one failed to conform, long familiar to me. Nobody can excel a Dutch bureaucrat in composing the most formal and ponderous of sentences that yet contrive to be violently, personally rude. What dismayed me in England was that the English forms were somehow like the English life, with a threadbare politeness and a false humility that I never understood. The summons, haughty and peremptory, to wait with bows and scrapes upon some petty functionary, which was signed "Your obedient servant"! Being a stranger, I found, made one automatically an inferior. Still, I remember England with gratitude; it was there that I learned to go to concerts.

Youth ended, as it began, with a fiasco. At the end of my postgraduate course, I went for my first real holiday—to Paris. I had money in my pocket, and a falsely bold sense of freedom. Alas, how provincial I felt myself. I had thought of my French as good, and discovered it to be pitiful. I had thought I would feel at home in Paris. Had I not often heard my parents recall happy times there? My mother had been to a Parisian finishing school. Later she had shopped at Lanvin and Hermès in the Rue Saint Honoré. My father had often said that the only ties he could wear without feeling sick were those from Sulka. My parents had not felt as lumpish as I did.

More humiliations followed. I tried to get into an expensive restaurant and was told there was no table, then fancied I could hear the aproned waiters laugh. I got into another, though, could not understand the menu, and was served a dish I was unable to digest, with a sauce of pounded shellfish and brandy I thought revolting. I ordered a half bottle of wine; they brought me a whole one that I did not know how to refuse. With my Dutch notions, it seemed a crime to waste what had cost so much; I drank it all. I stumbled out somehow, and when the fresh air hit me outside, I just vomited everything upon the pavement.

In hospitals I was competent. I was a doctor; I was even regarded as brilliant. Why did the two halves of my life seem to slip apart? Why, outside, did I feel bitterly that I was still the boy who in Paris stared at the statues in the Luxembourg and was only reminded of childhood and pictures of those statues, young girls by Rodin, that had spurred on that agonized wish to know, to possess, to understand these mystery-shrouded female figures?

16

I find I have stayed up, writing all this out—should I say spitting it all out?—till well after midnight. I have gone to bed here in my tower, in Casimir's aerie, secure from interruption or irritation, but I cannot sleep. I have stirred too much among dregs that I had thought settled and finally hardened. Muddy clouds have swirled to the surface and left me with an unexpected bitter aftertaste. It is pointless now to tear all this up. I yielded to some compulsion to scribble it down—as though that could do me or anyone else any good— and now I will leave it.

But I will stop here. I am not, after all, going to tell you about my early manhood, about Beatrix and why I married her, how I came to acquire and build up this practice, how—or why—I began to seduce my female patients, nor about the unexpected, astonishing successes I have had in so doing. You will just have to use what wits you have.

17

You are continuing your quiet subterranean war. I see by the book you have phoned up again for an appointment.

Indeed, Miss Maas commented upon it.

"As far as I understand," she said, "this is some police official. I rather think he's concealing whatever's wrong with him from his office people; he seems unwilling to accept appointments in advance, as though he were afraid of being found out." She smiled tolerantly. "I imagine he's putting on a good face in front of his world, terrified they should discover he was ill."

"Is he awkward?" I asked indifferently.

"No. But he asks for the afternoon of the same day in a soft pleading voice, as though he knew that only then could he slip off undisturbed. I asked Mrs. Marks whether she minded changing. I knew she wouldn't; she has nothing to do but go to the hairdresser."

Miss Maas sees nothing odd in this; the eccentricities

of patients are the small change of her day. I see, of course, other reasons for your conduct. Oh yes, Mr. van der Valk, I do indeed think that you are concealing things from your superior officers. Whatever the evidence is that you certainly possess, you are sitting on it very quietly.

For some reason of your own, and to do you justice I think it is more than a pretense of playing cat and mouse, you are moving with extreme caution around me. Is it that you really have nothing sound to go on at all? Or is it, which I think more likely, that you have too much, and cannot dislodge me without stirring up a scandal that would cause heads to roll, involving, as it would, altogether too many important personages? One of my fortifications is the number of well-known patients I treat discreetly—as I do you. I have a member of the government who gets headaches. He is quite as wary and quite as surreptitious as you are about appointments, which he makes himself; not even his secretary is allowed to know that he consults me.

Or Mrs. Marks . . . she is the soul of virtue, wife of the owner of a firm that is a household word. If there were, later, talk about my female patients, woe to him that began it. I am quite sure that you cannot arrest me.

Yet you press upon my weak spots. When you came today, and I had the last pages I wrote still fresh in my mind, I thought that you knew already more than is good for you. You sat, as has become your habit, on the sofa, took out a cigarette and fiddled with it, sniffed happily at the flowers, looked at me with the expression women's magazines would call "quizzical."

206

I looked quizzical right back. I, too, looked at the flowers. I am fond of flowers, but not the carnations and lilies and orchids of the plate-glass palaces, which I rather hate. The shopgirls pick them out to fill our standing order twice a week. I prefer field flowers, those my father painted. They do not last if they are cut, but growing they remind me of the roadsides of France, and not of the rarefied glass prisons where Dutch flowers are reared. Of Suzanne, and not of Beatrix.

I did not fiddle with my cigarette; I put it in my mouth and lit it with a crocodile-and-gold lighter, a present from Beatrix, bought—yes—on the Rue Saint Honoré in Paris. She frequently goes to Paris, where she studies New Looks, New Waves, and New Nonsense. You were plainly leaving me to move the first pawn today.

"My poor Van der Valk, aren't you getting a little owlish?"

"How so?" you said with your grin; you enjoy remarks like this.

"Surely you have realized by now that whatever extraordinary imaginary misdeeds you have lodged in your head, you cannot possibly prove anything at all."

"That isn't what worries me," you said quite seriously.

"No? Then I fail to see what does worry you. I feel a duty toward you, since you are inscribed on a folder as my patient."

" 'Worries me,' " you repeated thoughtfully, struck by the word. "Now, why did I say 'worries'? I'm worrying about that. Yes—you. You worry me."

"I do? Tell me, then; I'm interested in this symptom."

"That's good, that's very good—that you should be interested. I was afraid you'd continue to pretend boredom."

"Stop acting."

You advanced suddenly on the double, your bayonet fixed. "I find you spend too much time in your tower above here. I find you too apart from everything. What contact have you, after all, with the world? You read papers, you will tell me, books, periodicals. You keep up with medicine. You see plenty of people. And between you and all these things I find a barrier. You're too far away altogether. Reaching you isn't going to be easy." You shook your head sadly and made a casual dab at the ash tray, exactly as though you had said, "I wish it would rain. All this dryness does the crops no good."

I was irritated, naturally. I had to check this irritation. "My poor fellow, you have seen me here three times, and you have, I suppose, ferreted out any information in the public domain. I suppose you have a questioned my friends. And you have the impudence to come here and talk like this?"

"Oh, no, I don't question your friends. They'd all be curious immediately; it would be most unwise. No no, just the public domain. I've seen you, of course, more than three times. You show too little interest in me. Shall I give you an example?"

"Do."

"You go every week to the athletic club. Tuesday evenings, unless there's a concert you particularly wish not to miss. You take this exercise seriously. You never have evening appointments"—smiling in an irritating fashion at the evening appointments—"on Tuesdays. You play squash, at which you're quite an adept. With two or three friends, doctors like you. The little weekly health cure."

"There is no mystery or secret about that. Come to the point," I said.

"Why, it is just a coincidence that I go there, too, and even play squash sometimes. I haven't followed you; I've gone there for years. Yet you have no notion of that. Your eyes are shut. Last week I practically trod on your feet and you never gave me a glance. You have a wish—which I feel is a bad wish—to obliterate the world, dismiss it from your presence."

I had no immediate answer. I was, indeed, taken aback. It is true that squash on Tuesdays is an old habit of mine, and it is true that I know few people there. There are separate groups, though—the fencers, for instance, to whom the club really belongs. I did not offer excuses, which would have sounded feeble. "I can't say that my not noticing you at a place where I go for exercise rather than conversation is much of an indictment."

"Who said anything about an indictment? A straw. Take another straw, if you like. The day you were kind enough to show me your tower, where you are so delightfully away from the sweaty mob, like me, I glanced at your bedside books. What do I find? Fantasies. Totally imaginary worlds."

I will admit that you do not leer, as though you think yourself clever. But these were half truths, difficult to admit, pointless to deny. I am indeed fond of those stories (an amazing mythological romance by some talented Englishman, a professor of philology or some such science, for he has a great sense of words). They are splendid bedside reading. There is no earthly reason to be ashamed of them, and of course to say that liking such books shows a desire to escape from reality is utterly groundless and absurd, the very worst kind of amateur pretend-psychiatry. I said as much tartly. And you laughed heartily.

"The observation," you said with odious amusement, "was a trial balloon, sent up to see if you would shoot at it. Of course your liking for a book—and I don't care if it's *Justine* or *Alice in Wonderland*—is not in the least an ominous fact. But that you should rush so warmly to your own defense over it shows me that you are aware that there is truth in what I say. The straws are connected with a lot of others, which I don't see. I'll give you a very cunning analogy that has just occurred to me. If you wish to give a quick elementary test to my nervous system, you tap me on the knee to see if I jerk. That's exactly what I've just done. Tapped you on the knee. It jerked. Shall we try another?" You were full of a kind of childish enjoyment that I have noticed is a favorite pose of yours; I refrain from drawing superficial conclusions about your character.

"Your analogy is false, and your pretended knowledge of an inexact science is zero," I said crossly. "A dabble of jargon that lays bare your superficial mind."

"Very very good. Shall we try something else? Your foot—what's the jargon word, now, for tickling someone's foot and seeing if the toes curl? Mine curl like a bloody octopus at the bare thought."

I had to smile, too. "A simple reaction test," I said

gravely, "known to the ignorant, like you, as the Babinski reflex, after a French neurologist of more distinction than myself."

"Babinski—isn't that perfect? Can't go wrong with a name like that. Well, now—I'm perfectly serious— I invite you for a little game of squash. Not Tuesday —how about Thursday? You'll beat me easily. Do your toes curl?"

It was, I think, your irritating smile that provoked me. You were watching me closely, I saw, for signs of hesitation or irritation. "Why not?" I said agreeably. "And now I will ask you to excuse me; I see by my little light that I have a patient waiting."

18

I have thought quite a good deal about you since that last scrap of conversation. I am thinking, to be exact, about a science as inexact, to be sure, and as distorted by popular prejudice in the public mind as psychiatry. You are not a pretentious person, and I think you would disclaim any scientific basis in criminology. There are theories, I gather, that are probably taught to aspiring policemen at the training school. I suspect that you would agree that these are as outdated as the measuring of bumps on men's heads.

As a neurologist, I have a slight prejudice against psychiatry, because of the popular confusion. People are constantly coming to me and asking gravely whether psychoanalysis would help them. I notice that the courts, in criminal cases, tend to rely more and more upon psychiatric opinions. I myself would not care to be the consultant expected to give a serious opinion upon an old woman who has poisoned both her husbands with weed killer in a twenty-year interval. I take this as an example since there have lately been two or three remarkably similar examples of this reported in the press. Parathion has become a bogyman: there is now no man, woman, or child in Holland that does not know how to buy it, how to administer it, and that the Minister is studying ways of restricting the open unimpeded sale of this disagreeable chemical. One does not need to be a psychiatrist to know that there will be several more cases.

I do not believe that any serious psychiatric practitioner will really have the insolent vanity to pretend that he can reach into these old women, and say with certainty, "This is the monster that the prosecutor claims, and it is your duty, gentlemen, to apply rigorous methods." Equally, he would be very rash to say, "Give her to me in the clinic for a year, and I will restore you a balanced and useful member of society." He knows that both answers are nonsense. He cannot do that old woman the faintest good.

Even the physiological aspects of human pain and misery are dreadfully obscure. I am a skillful and sensitive diagnostician, but I am singularly helpless in an alarming number of instances. There are men, certainly, who have trained themselves by rigorous disciplines to a sensitivity even greater than that of the complex and delicate machinery we rely upon. An example made familiar by the publicity he was forced to yield to is that of Felix Kersten. But Kersten himself, able to reach and relieve the stomach-aches of Heinrich Himmler, could not put an end to them.

You, Van der Valk, will agree with me that in a

given set of circumstances any man will commit a crime. Because of a disturbed nervous system. When fears and anxieties begin to press upon a man, an endless series of permutations produces a criminal. The causes of this nervous stress . . . my poor friend. Snobbery, for instance, and the spirit of competition. The fear of age that is the result of our newly learned overstated deference toward youth. What are the effects—the physiological effects—of the human conscience, that abominable invention, upon the human body? You will certainly tell me that for every man I show you who is ill you could show me a criminal.

Are we all criminals? Has every exaggerated-seeming manifestation of the human spirit a nervous origin? Was Jeanne d'Arc simply a witch? Are all saints neurotics, deranged, dangerous persons, because their neurosis has become disabling, psychotic? Was the Protestant religion, for example, caused by nothing more than Martin Luther's chronic constipation or John Calvin's earaches? You see at once that the theory is ridiculous. We cannot oversimplify. There is much more to it than a physiological explanation.

I do not use the word religion in its narrow, sectarian sense. In all the doings and thoughts of humanity there is a moral problem. All drama moves upon a moral pivot—a truism. This moral sense—if infected, will a criminal inevitably appear? What is a criminal?

Let us suppose, in accordance with your often-indulged fantasy, that you are, my dear Van der Valk, a neurologist. To be concrete, you are Felix Kersten, called upon to treat Heinrich Himmler for excruciating and disabling pains—the famous S.S. stomach-

213

ache. You observe this patient at length, over a period of years. You find a moral person. Himmler had antique military virtues that have become, in our society, derisive. Loyal, honest, incorruptible, patriotic. Poor in money despite his position. Generous, kind to the poor, devoted to the family. His ideals were simplicity, self-sacrifice, integrity. Nobody denies all this.

Should not the whole world have respected such a man? He himself could never understand that there could exist people who would not respect him.

The conventional and the stupid have defined Himmler as a monstrous criminal. Other, learned gentlemen have said he was nothing of the sort, but that he was a little school-master, slightly crazy in the way many persons are who would not harm a fly but who hold strange theories about the Lost Tribes of Israel.

You know—you, Kersten, the neurologist—that the stomache-ache is caused by forcing the little schoolmaster to do monstrous things. But they are not, to him, monstrous. . . . You see, the exact nature of illness, and of crime, eludes you.

Kersten was a very skillful, very sensitive, wonderfully equipped doctor, to whom I would be an ignorant journeyman.

Am I ill? Am I a criminal? I wish you knew. You do not know, because if you knew you would arrest me. This business of evidence is unimportant, really, isn't it?

Has it something to do with God? What God? That lunatic old Stalinist despot? The gentle lamb with the woolly beard and the bleeding heart in the middle of the spotless white robe? The God of Islam, of the desert, of the romantic Garden of Allah, with its oil

214

borings surrounded by jeeps, guarded by paratroops, and with fresh asparagus flown in each week by Air France?

Whose God? Whom does God belong to, in Holland? An anecdote . . . The other day I was accosted by one of those girls in the street with evangelist tracts. It is disgraceful to be rude to someone with the courage to stand in the street and voice unpopular or ridiculous opinions. I did not stop her buttonholing me, but I have no use for tracts.

"It is in aid of one or another sect, isn't it? There are too many, you know."

She agreed at once, surprising me. A grave girl, quite young, not pretty but with fine eyes. I'm afraid, she said, that is quite true. There are a hundred and eighteen in this country alone.

Did you know that, Van der Valk? Quite likely you do; you are a perfect wastebasket of unlikely pieces of knowledge.

I belong to no sects, of course. What infuriated me was that the girl was a great deal less perturbed about it than I would be. Did that elusive God invent crime? I bring no peace, he said; I bring a sword.

19

I read over what I wrote the other night. About my childhood. No psychiatrist, except a fool, hidebound by ridiculous rules (which all vary according to the school he went to), would pretend to find the sources there of my adult character, my beliefs and decisions, my characteristic behavior. Even if he knew more, even if I told him about my adult life. There would be too many oversimplifications.

I do not believe any doctor capable of penetrating the human being. Imagine a perfect doctor, possessing the arts of the psychiatrist, the science of the physiologist, the skill of the neurologist, and the experience of mankind and his liver that the old-fashioned general practitioner has. Imagine him read in the knowledge of the Chinese, the Arabs, the Persians. Give him all the latest equipment developed by research teams in Berkeley, California—bless their cotton socks.

Idiotic, is it not?

Very well, create a team of doctors uniting all these branches of knowledge. You would get a fine farce; they would be quarreling violently inside thirty seconds.

Vanity . . .

Do you remember that at the beginning of this manuscript I jokingly mentioned M. Simenon? He would do as well as any. We cannot bother him, alas; he is busy walking up and down his garden, five miles a day. A peripatetic philosopher. You will have to do. I would write to him, but I fear he has secretaries, and is pestered by lunatics, beggars, and would-be authors.

Am I a criminal, M. Simenon?

I am not an interesting person. Neurologically I belong to the common, fairly dull category of the overtense—*"les grands nerveux."* I need a quiet life, regular hours, plenty of food and sleep. I am at my best in the mornings. My reactions are poor. I have never dared drive a motor regularly. My muscles are weak, my digestion uncertain. Against this I am capable of considerable nervous energy and have a good

216

analytical mind. High intelligence and cramped muscles. I have a need for fresh air and exercise, and plenty of massage. Something like M. Voltaire—or should we say Herr Himmler? I have few mental weaknesses; I am neither lazy, envious, nor gluttonous. I have learned patience and detachment. I am resilient, agile, and receptive.

My body gives me little trouble, but I understand it. My internal organs are all present and in good condition. My eyes, ears, and teeth are all sound and sharp. I keep in adequate condition with a game of squash and a Finnish sauna each week. I take a winter-sport holiday each year, and a little villa on the coast of Portugal for a month every summer.

You will be puzzled about my wife. Perhaps you are right and this is the great failure of my life. The catastrophe, possibly, that cracked the criminal open. Beware, my friend, of worldly ambition. You know all this already? How deeply have you observed me?

A thought strikes me. I give every person who consults me a thorough physical examination. Never would I risk a diagnosis, even of acne (I have several patients with acne), without it. But you have to diagnose without this aid. You must make up the deficiency by observation. I wonder how good you are at this. It is because I am, I know, good at it that I am going to conduct this experiment. It will be salutary for you to read. I am going to see what it is I know about you—purely from observation.

That is all talk, nonsense, pretense. The truth is simply that I wish I knew you better.

I must rely upon memory. But my memory, both visual and aural, is excellent.

217

You are not as tall as I am, but I am only a hundred and eighty-five pounds. You are a lot broader, but you will get tubby, my friend, unless you take a good deal more exercise than I need. You weigh, I should guess, a hundred and eighty. I approve of your hands, which are strong, broad, and, I am glad to say, clean. I am more suspicious of your shirts. Do you prefer plain dark cotton shirts for themselves or because they show the dirt less? You are not dressy; your suits are cheap, but they look well on you. You do not, I am glad to say, wear sports jackets or blazers. Simple and suitable—it is a good point. Your shoes, though, are expensive—plain soft leather. Second good point.

Your face is a little too much that of an intelligent ape. It is harsh and bony, which makes it tolerable. Your jaw is too heavy, your teeth too big, your mouth too wide, with enormous furrows alongside it. Your nose is good. Your eyes are too small and too pale. You are good and broad between the ears, and your hair is nearly as short as mine—no lovelocks. If your forehead were less low and your jaw less prominent, and you had not that comedian's rubbery mouth, you might be quite bearable-looking.

When talking, you have a pleasant habit of taking your coat off and rolling up your sleeves; it is unselfconscious, has nothing to do with the warmth, and amuses me. Your wedding ring is narrow, and you are a Jansenist, I notice. You have a Seamaster watch—a present from your wife, no doubt; it is just the kind of watch one gets as a reward for being ten years married.

You rummage a great deal in your pockets, which are always full of rubbish. I have noticed a workmanlike pocketknife, your package of cigarettes that is always squashed (I agree that cigarette cases are detestable things), a kleptomaniac liking for rubber bands, paper clips, and pieces of string. You are no truster of ball-point pens, since you have always at least three, yet you go on—trustingly—buying cheap ones. You keep your money in a purse—pleasantly old-fashioned of you. You come, obviously, of a poor family and were trained as a child to be careful and waste nothing.

You are—I hazard the guess with confidence—largely self-educated. You have been to no superior school, no university. Do you rather resent people with that polytechnic gloss upon them? Yet you have a huge respect for it. If you were French, you would take your hat off in the Rue d'Ulm.

What you do have is considerable intellectual curiosity. You have read smatterings of poetry and philosophy. You know nothing about music but you are fairly well read. You speak French and German, a thing I envy, since I read both but cannot speak them. You have been—but that you told me yourself—in the army in England.

You are very Dutch. You have a characteristic crudeness, brutality. Your tendency toward lavatory humor is deplorable. You have Dutch virtues: stability, perseverance, obstinacy. You also have too much imagination altogether—less common, here—and you are absurdly individualist. You certainly behave toward me as no policeman under orders would; that, my friend, is your own, your personal idea.

You have a certain sympathy for me, which you take—good for you—little pains to conceal. You are

219

a bit of a sensualist yourself; you like eating and drinking, don't you? And girls, and perfume, and southern baroque art, and Mediterranean landscapes. You have a strong vulgar streak, and are not ashamed about it.

Damn you. Anybody else would never have penetrated my fortifications. I could have complained about you; you would not have cared.

I want you to know that I deliberately did not complain of you, and that I am not afraid of you. I wish to show you that I am in some sense worthy of you, that I do not lack all humor, that when you arrest me I shall not resent you. I rather like you, and I rarely like people. Did I say it earlier? We could, under other circumstances, have been friends.

I am wrong. It is just these circumstances that make us friends.

You have overcome your ingrained Dutch respect for my position. You do not think of me as a doctor. When you lay hands upon me, will it be the doctor or the person? I find it difficult to see you as the policeman, with nothing better to do in life than clapping malefactors into handcuffs.

I am envious of you. Of your combativeness, of your courage. The unorthodoxy that is your dominant trait interests me the more because of your position and function in our rigid social order. Here, where orthodoxy is expected and exacted, you have outflanked me. That takes courage. You belong to the hierarchy, and any shaky pillar in that hierarchy has small chance of survival. How do you defend the reputation for eccentricity you certainly possess?

My envy is the keener because I can speak with

authority. I belong to the structure I talk of. I am expected to be a pillar of society. It is exacted from me to behave as a doctor is expected to behave. That is an inelegant phrase, which will worry neither of us.

Of course, if we show combativeness we are not punished, as you are doubtless punished, by a reprimand, the famous and classic Dutch *berisping*. We are punished by a barely noticeable coolness. This drop in the temperature is accompanied by a drop in the income, for by a mysterious grapevine the patients are aware of the situation. "He may be good at curing your ailments, but he is not quite one of us; you might do better to avoid. . . ." Once upon this slippery slope, he had better begin to mend his ways, or he will find himself, unless he gets quickly and unobtrusively back into line, in much the same circumstances as a prominent man, let us say, in the state of Georgia, to whom has been attached the little label "nigger lover."

I think I know why you survive, why you have an advantage that I have not. I think that you possess not simply combativeness but talent. Talent, considerable talent, can secure one from persecution. I can think of perhaps half a dozen people who, possessing this talent, have secured their freedom. Even a minister. . . .

Have you understood why I have dwelt at length on this subject, why I am so fascinated by this spectacle? Quite right, my friend. It is because I myself fail. I do not belong to your club, the club of those who have talent, who do not care. I do not have enough talent. I am not good enough.

Naturally, I do not fall into the obvious error of self-pity, or that of underestimating my capacities. Nor do I wish you to think that I throw all the blame upon my wife. It is true that I have thought things might have turned out very differently had I married another woman, but that is not Beatrix's fault. I chose her. I married her deliberately, in cold blood, for the affluence, for the position, for the introduction she could give me into what I thought of as "the club." *Le tout-Paris.* I had not understood then that there is only one club.

And I am a good doctor. But I have never broken through the barrier that separates the people with skill from the winner. I am a born second-rater, a born lightweight. Perhaps you have not yet found this out.

But you will.

20

I am discouraged. You eluded me. I thought that we had reached a point . . . that we were going to make real contact at last. You delighted me, and then you eluded me.

I went to the athletic club, but with the feeling that I was making a mistake, that I should be bored, that I might make even a fool of myself. What have I to do with you, after all? You are, at the end of the reckoning, a two-bit policeman who thinks himself clever. You are no cleverer than I am, perhaps less so. You do not get to me except insofar as I allow you to, amusedly, to let you see what you miss, how wide you are and remain of the mark. I have tempted you to think yourself more clever than you are. But you are a clown, Inspector Thing, and a clown does not entrap a person like myself. You know that you cannot proceed against me, and you propose, impudently, that I should yield to you. . . .

It was an odd sensation, arriving in a place you are familiar with and finding it so unfamiliar. I had not realized that the Thursday clientele would be so different from that of Tuesday. I suppose there are sporting fanatics who haunt the place, but they are not interesting to me. I felt lost, and wandered about wondering whether you had already arrived. I was recognized by no one but the woman who makes coffee behind the bar, and all she said was "Why, hello, Doctor, lost your calendar?" That annoyed me.

I found you gossiping with a man I neither know nor wish to know; he looks a clot. You told me he was regarded as a serious contender in the lightweights, or the featherweights, or the clotweights, for the European Judo Championships—as though I cared. You were learning, you said, about judo in case you got the sack from the police and had to take a job as a taxi driver; this was for my benefit. Your clotweight pal, who had the type of very curly close straw hair that sets my teeth on edge, thought this was a good joke and clapped you on the back. If people clap me on the back, I simply do not speak to them again, but a policeman, I suppose, cannot afford such gestures. The man looked to me the sort of bank clerk that absconds with funds, but perhaps that is why you cultivate his acquaintance.

You had to gossip some more with another pal, a fat girl with rattail hair and a moronic look—a swimmer. After keeping me waiting a good twenty minutes, you said, "Well, let's go and play squash," and I was

223

so irritated that it took me several minutes to regain my control.

I changed; there are only a few clothes lockers in this place, and I have one, though I take my playing clothes home each time after use. Clothes that have been sweated in, after hanging a day in a closed locker, smell most unpleasant; it is a pity other people do not recognize this fact. The squash court, though the fencers use it as well, is the only place on the premises that does not smell of feet.

I changed into cotton trousers and a track-suit top. You sprawled on a bench with your hands in the pockets of denim shorts; you had simply taken off your trousers and dumped them. It irritates me to have someone watch me change, but it was a good exercise in the kind of watchful calm I have to maintain with you.

I do not wear shorts except when I am swimming; I have the kind of stringy leg that does not look well in shorts. You, I noticed, had exactly the kind of loose muscular leg, rather too hairy, that does look at its best in precisely the brief shorts you wore. You see that I have acquired a habit—your habit—of observation.

To make conversation, for a stony silence had fallen and I am not talkative in my underpants in public, I said something trivial. Your white sweater—rather off-white, if I may say so, and you might ask your wife to wash it—was ordinary, but I needed something ordinary to restore my even quietness.

"Nice sweater."

You beamed with your childish enjoyment. "Isn't it. Standard Navy issue to submarine crews; cost me two-fifty twenty years ago in a government surplus store in Gosport."

224

Typical.

I took my racket out of its press; yours wasn't in a press. "I have any number of balls."

"Delighted to hear it. I haven't any; my children pinch them."

We walked onto the court. I am a fair squash player, having a sensitive touch. If I play a ball into an angle, I generally get the return angle I want. I stand still as much as I can, because I can't chase balls. I saw that I could beat you straight off on skill alone, but you gave me a harder match than I had thought. Once you took your sweater off (you had an ordinary cotton street shirt on), you started chasing everything. Hitting far too hard at impossible balls, talking, laughing, catcalling, jumping up and down when, as you quite often did, you brought off a good return with a shot that cannoned all over the court and left me flatfooted. You ran like a wild man, crashed into walls, sent half your services out of court, played one or two cunning flick shots I had not thought you capable of, and at least three superb balls that nobody could have returned, even though next time, invariably, you missed the ball altogether and looked accusingly at your racket to see where the hole was. As for my play, it was like myself —clever, controlled, occasionally extremely skillful.

I find myself—probably momentarily, certainly temporarily—a thought depressed. I am tired. I find you like the Old Man of the Sea. I need a break from my routine. I have thought that this would be a mistake in tactics, as it might lead you to imagine that the strain was telling on me, but I do not care what you think. Thinking things will not help you find legal or convincing proof against me.

I have been tempted, at times of fatigue like this, to slash the whole knot apart conclusively. I could always disappear. You have, no doubt, eyes upon me. You could arrange, possibly, to be notified if I made any unusual withdrawals from the bank. No, that, I rather think, is an official act needing official sanction, and I have never believed that you had any official sanction. Yes, it it a temptation to think of the pleasant life I could construct in South America.

Come, come. That sounds too much like some deplorable doctor who has made revolting experiments in concentration camps. I must not become childish. I have all the weaknesses of a member of the "establishment" and all the strengths. No police officer will dare institute a process against me. You would be bedeviled by a perfect tidal wave of outrage. Wrongful arrest, slander, damage to professional standing, abusive and excessive use of judicial powers. I have only to lift a finger, ring my Minister, say that I am being blackmailed by a police officer.

My position is extremely strong, for as long as I choose to keep it so. I feel better; I always pick up rapidly. I will go off for a week, and you cannot do a damn thing about it. Not to the sea, I think; the season is still too summery and there are tourists everywhere. Perhaps the forests. Autumn is getting near, and there will soon be mushrooms. I am tempted by the notion of trees, huge numbers of trees, and I could pick a few amanitas for you, as a present.

That game of squash was typical of Post, thought Van der Valk, taking off his shorts and stuffing them in his briefcase, next to the gray cardboard file marked

226

"C.M.P." He beat me, of course, being a practiced, clever player. Yet if I took this damn game seriously, I could beat him. By chasing everything, pushing him, playing him off balance, pressing in on him—if I practiced . . . Sure he is a tricky player, but when the ball flies out of his reach, he lets it go. Smiling slightly, he stands aloof watching it go, and gives his opponent that faint nod of amused congratulation, as though one were a peasant beneath his notice. As though there were something contemptible about running, fighting, competing. There's no fight in him.

It was at that moment that Van der Valk decided to lash out for all he was worth.

He waited for the Doctor in the bar. "How about a drink? Not here—too many people. Why not in the Amstel? That's more your style anyway. Quiet, discreet, elegant, beautiful view over the water at evening. Twilight on the bridge—Whistler nocturne—that's what we like about the Amstel, that nostalgic feeling. No police riffraff there, either." The Amstel Hotel, which is the best in Holland, was a couple of hundred yards away, along the Sarphatistraat.

"Very well," said Post agreeably. "It might be pleasant. I quite enjoy your company. You make an interesting study, too—do you know you're quite a casebook example?"

Van der Valk beamed at him. "Still waiting for me to get tired and go home and leave you in peace?"

"That is your choice. It is your time you waste. It is a matter of indifference to me. Have I not told you about the man who used to get a recurrent desire to kill me?"

"Here we are. We might meet Mr. Merckel; this is

a great stamping ground for your patients. Official dinners, with miniature decorations, under the gracious patronage of royalty. Preserving wildlife, or some such praiseworthy cause."

They sat down by the window that overlooks the terrace and looked out at the Amstel River.

"I buy the drinks, since I lost the game. Two very good very large cognacs."

"Certainly, sir. Any special brand?"

"Whatever you please. And two Cuban cigars."

"Police hospitality!" said Post. "I'm quite struck. Rather significant, I fear—compensation wishes in you. Why not two beers and a package of Caballeros?"

"You're a very special customer of mine. I like to see them happy, too. Look at him warming the glasses —he gets bored, you know. Like me. I have sympathy for all waiters; I'm sort of a one myself."

"Speaking for myself, I'm never bored."

"You aren't? Here's to you. I got this for you really because you need it." Van der Valk smiled.

"What, after a game of squash? A glass of squash, more likely."

"This is different. Now we're in a championship match. You want to absorb a lot of courage. You know who wins championship matches? The one who survives setbacks the longest. If that game had been for a championship, I'd have beaten you easily, wouldn't I? You follow?"

Post said nothing. Van der Valk picked up the enormous glass, stood it on his nose, put it down and licked his lips happily. "I must be off; my wife will be wondering where I've got to. Though I think I'll take a little stroll back along the river as far as the Rem-

228

brandtplein. Smoke this as I go. They taste best along the waterside."

"Good night."

"My pleasure. Ring me up sometime . . . when you've had enough of it. Don't get like Casimir—you'll start collecting younger and younger girls. . . . No future in it. You'd really like to be free of that house, too, wouldn't you? You can, you know. So long."

Rather wearily, Post caught the waiter's eye and ordered another brandy. He heartily wished that he was back in his studio, lying in his silk dressing gown on the cheap divan with a book. Jane Austen—he was getting to enjoy Jane Austen. . . .

It was with some glee that Van der Valk heard about Dr. van der Post's little holiday in the Schwarzwald. That was a good sign—nothing like a good German introspective forest landscape to bring out one's melancholy poetic nature. One renounced women for the little volume of Rilke bound in limp leather. Or, of course, one took one's rifle and went deer hunting. Even better! Post in the role of hunter would be fine; he would spend a good deal of time sympathizing with the deer. What thoughts would pass through his mind at the moment when, after a long crawl through sodden bracken, he finally got downwind of an unsuspecting beast, found a sight line, saw the cross hairs on his backsight wavering across that rough warm sympathetic flank, loosened all his muscles, breathing shallowly through the mouth, and waited for the rifle barrel to steady on the sturdy muscled shoulder? Would he really be able to feel the skin tighten and whiten on the top knuckle of the right hand?

Whatever the fellow did, he, Van der Valk, busy deer hunting in a smelly little office in the Marnixstraat, would be thinking up some new medicine to tighten the screw still more. He had at the moment no good idea how, but he would find one—oh yes.

Unfortunately he got tangled suddenly in one of the incomprehensibly busy periods of a policeman's life. Instead of pleasant summery evenings observing the demeanor of the art whore, he was getting home at eleven at night, dulled and silent, to be given cocoa and rolled toward his bed by a wife he did not see at all during the day and hardly saw now when she dragged his socks off and pulled his shirt out of his belt to tap his back muscles loose. Not for the first time, he was forced to forget all about Dr. van der Post. There were other pots that might come to the boil if he stoked hard enough.

All the same, it was Chief Inspector Kan who finally got Cross-Eyed Janus after he had made the grievous mistake of getting overambitious. If he had stuck to secondhand cars, they would never have reached him, but Janus was tired of being a garage attendant. He wanted to be a gentleman. Damn it, there were criminals a lot worse than he to whom the Public Prosecutor took his hat off when he saw them on the street. Janus made an unwary phone call. When Kan called, prim and tidy, Janus, who had always thought Kan a good subject for a horselaugh, was disconcerted. Worse, he lost his head. He offered Kan a big bribe—they were all quite startled how big, and if it had been anybody but Kan, they would have suspected him of exaggerating. Poor old Janus—all that money, and his looks against him, and the fearful Amsterdam accent, and those Charing Cross Road clothes. He should never have got friendly with Rouppe, who looked like a gentleman and even behaved like one, so that Janus had never imagined he might be a police informer.

They had him. Issuing of false written statements (a great Dutch catchall), incomplete and falsified income-tax returns, receiving of goods known to be stolen, harboring of same, attempted disposal of same, interfering with an officer in the execution of his duty, attempted corruption of a state functionary—the Officer of Justice (sunburned around his receding hairline after a delightful holiday in the Aegean) made a little addition of penalties, arrived at a fantastic total, and rather regretfully concluded that a lot of these sentences would have to run concurrently.

The police department was jubilant. They were being jubilant when the telephone rang.

"For you, Van der Valk."

"Gentleman asking to speak to you," said the concierge at the switchboard.

"Well, we're all gentlemen today," handsomely. "Put him on. Does the gentleman have a name."

"A Dr. Post." Van der Valk had a tiny shock of guilt at having forgotten, and gave himself a rap on the knuckle of his trigger finger. His deer was within range, and he had been busy badger watching.

"Van der Valk. Good morning to you. No, this is a private line. Yes, I'm alone in the office." The others were gawking, but they held their tongues.

"Would you care to come and see me in my consulting room when you can spare the time?" Post said, his quiet voice sounding remote and cool, as unemotional as ever. A pause. "Are you still there?"

"Certainly I'm still here," Van der Valk said. "I was thinking. I'd be inclined to make another suggestion. Suppose you came to see me here?"

"There? In that Headquarters Building, or whatever you call it?" Post sounded a little shocked at this invasion of privacy.

"I believe—I base this on the experience of a good many people—you'd find this a great deal easier in my office than in yours. We'd be perfectly private, and undisturbed. Simply ask at the desk for Commissaris Samson's office. I'll see that the concierge does not keep you waiting."

There was another pause, at Post's end this time. "Why do you suggest this?" he asked, at last.

The answer, thought Van der Valk, would be important. "That terrible house," he said. "Wait a minute, I'm looking for the right way to express myself." Van der Valk's eye glanced around the room. Mr. Kan was already busy making notes on the margin of a report. Mr. Samson was sitting—or, rather, standing with his backside propped against a table, his hands in his pockets, watching. He had a faint grin, as though curious to see how Van der Valk would handle this.

"Perhaps the best way of putting it is to say that once you are here, you can shed, completely, an identity that has grown distasteful. The gestures we go through here are almost totally automatic and impersonal. We no longer have any hostility, you see. If anything, it's rather a friendly performance."

The pause this time was slighter. "Are you free at this minute? I mean, to be more precise, in about twenty minutes?"

232

"Free as the wind."

"Very well," suddenly. "You can expect me."

Van der Valk put the phone down and said "Oof!"

"Post, if I'm not much mistaken," said the old gentleman.

"Quite right. In a quarter of an hour. I'd like to make it easy for him."

Mr. Samson had understood. "Very well. In my office, then. You can be stenographer. So—he's realized at last that he's without a friend in the world?"

"He's realized, I think," said Van der Valk soberly, "that I'm the only one he's got."

ABOUT THE AUTHOR

NICOLAS FREELING was born in London and raised in France and England. After his military service in Europe, he traveled extensively throughout Europe, working as a professional cook in a number of hotel and restaurants. His first book, *Love in Amsterdam,* was published in 1961. Since then, he has written seventeen novels and two non-fiction works. His most recent books have been *Gadget,* a novel of suspense, and the third Henri Castang novel, *Sabine.* Mr. Freeling was awarded a golden dagger by the Crime Writers in 1963, the Grand Prix de Roman Policier in 1965, and the Edgar Allen Poe Award of the Mystery Writers Association in 1966.

Mr. Freeling lives in France with his wife and their five children.